FALLING FOR RED

ELENOR POUNTAIN

Contents

Author's Note

<u>Content Warnings</u>

Detailed sexual scenes and some detailed and implied abuse may trigger some readers. For more information on trigger warnings, please visit my website: elenor-pountain.com/trigger-warnings

Dedication

To my husband…
You're the Gavin to my Jess, the Ed to my Kiera and the Paul to
my Sophie. My biggest supporter, cheerleader and sounding
board… xx

FALLING FOR RED

Prologue

SOPHIE

Darkness is clawing in as I squeeze my eyes shut; it's consuming me as the cloud of black blocks out any light that is filtering through my eyelids. The sweat and tears are cooling my aching body and sliding down my cheeks as I struggle to fight against the shadow swallowing me whole.

A flutter of light breaks through, turning the black to grey. It's at this moment I swear to myself I won't let him hurt me anymore. My hand feels the cool wall behind me as I use it for support to stand, albeit shakily.

"Sophie…" His tone is sharp. My body tenses and I can no longer hear myself breathe.

It's okay, Sophie. Walk away now. You can do this!

The voice in my head is stronger than I am, but this has to stop.

"No, no more. You can't keep hurting me like this." My breathing is starting to regulate as I become more confident with my conviction. I can feel my heartbeat returning to normal and my strength coming back to me. He rolls his eyes at me, his strong, muscular frame edging closer as he towers over me.

"You've only done 3 reps; we've got 7 more to go. You signed up for PT sessions!"

I walk away from Justin; I don't care about the rest of the hour's money. I literally can't keep doing this to myself, especially when all I want is a buttery pastry and a giant latte. Grabbing my stuff from the locker room, I don't bother to change before I walk out of the gym and head straight across the street to Starbucks before I walk home.

Fuck the gym.

I strut down the street with my coffee in hand and my pastry begging me to get home quicker so I can devour it. During my torture session, my phone blew up. It's a Saturday morning, yet my phone never stops with requests, emails, and the occasional personal text. I work harder than anyone else in my firm. Being in a predominantly male environment, it's taken me longer than it should have to become a senior architect. You'd think in this day and age, your gender shouldn't matter, but it does. They're just better at hiding why you don't get the promotions you deserve…in some companies, anyway.

I get home and decide to wash off the stale smell of the gym before finishing my coffee and starting on my cinnamon roll. Sitting at my desk, I open my laptop and start on the emails from customers and management. To say I dislike my boss is an understatement.

He's not a bad person; he seems nice enough, but as a manager… He is absolutely terrible. Unless you have a dick, he's not interested in laughing with you or listening to your ideas. I created one of my best designs for a client, a modern smart house with beautiful landscaping to go with it. He didn't even consider it as one of the designs to pass on to them. It was only by mistake they saw my drawing on my desk when they'd been in for a meeting, and they asked him why they hadn't seen it. The lying bastard said he hadn't seen it before. I don't know what his problem is, but I feel like a woman has done him harm somewhere in his past for him to look over and down on me so much.

When I applied for senior architect for the first time three years ago, I wasn't given the job. Josh, someone who'd barely crawled out of their mother's womb with no experience, got the role instead. I call him Crayon's in my head because he should be drawing with crayons.

I should have left then, but this is one of the best architectural firms to work for if I want to further my career. I applied again a year later, but I didn't get it then either; someone whose daddy had influence got the job. When I applied last year, I was adamant that I'd be speaking to Citizens Advice if I didn't get it. However, when I got the job, I was ninety per cent sure it was because the only other applicant was a cocky intern who thought their Micky Mouse drawings were the dogs' bollox. A three-year-old could have done better with melted crayons.

Still, I'm here, working my ass off to prove to them

that I'm worthy of my title. If I'm being honest with myself, I'm worthy of doing my boss's job, but he's not going anywhere. He's in too tight with the powers that be. My dream is to have my own company. I would then get to choose my clients and the work. We have a variety of clients, but none of them really require much creativity. I want to sketch buildings that change the landscape of London. Beautiful, smart buildings that allow greenery to grow, rather than a concrete and glass jungle, and although I'd work just as hard and just as many hours, it would be for myself not to make sure I'm not judged for not pulling my weight.

As I'm finishing up after four hours of working, I see a calendar invite pop up for a team drink at the pub next week. I don't normally attend. As one of the only women in the small company of forty, apart from the receptionist, it's uncomfortable because they seem to think I'm deaf and can't hear their sexist remarks.

"Damn, look at that ass today."

"Jesus, her tits are spilling out of her bra. What I wouldn't do to that."

"It's a dog-eat-dog industry. Do you think they'd eat each other out?"

Shit like that prevents me from spending my personal time with them.

Just as I'm about to decline the invite, pretending I have an appointment, I get a personal email from my boss.

Sophie,

It'd be nice to see you at this event. Your personal life has

*been busy, and you haven't been able to make team
drinks.*
Richard

Dick. Huffing loudly, I click accept and respond to his email advising I'm actually free that evening. I have a feeling I'm going to regret this.

Chapter One

PAUL

I'm standing in my shower, body aching nicely from last night's activities, and whatever-her-name-is is getting dressed. I don't like them to hang around. They are always made aware it's a one-night deal and nothing more. The water is hot, and I enjoy the feeling of my muscles relaxing as I finish up. As I step out of my ensuite into the bedroom, I can see she's gone, but there is a little note on my pillow.

I really enjoyed last night. If you want to hook up again, you have my number.
Helen xx

I toss it in the bin, get dressed, and head into the office. I honestly don't have time for a relationship, and if she wants to hook up again, no matter how much fun I'd have, I know just from that note that she wants more, which is why I won't see her again.

I'm sitting at my desk, scrolling through emails and reports when I get a message from Gavin to say he wants to meet to discuss the Christmas party budget, and I'm concerned. He never has time for this stuff and normally leaves it to me, so naturally, we meet at the bar. I'm not buying that this is all the meeting is about.

We have a usual table in a quiet corner where we sit where we aren't disturbed, and our conversations can't be overheard either. We like to catch up here and discuss business as well as what little personal lives we have.

Gavin and I have a couple of drinks as we discuss the Christmas party. This year we're holding it at the Tower Hotel. He's also set aside a nice little budget for a pay raise and bonus for his new PA. The CEO I knew in the past was such a dick to his PAs that they never lasted long. This one not only impressed him, but she's also managed to get under his skin somehow. We talked about how we could adjust her role to give her more responsibility, as she really is an asset to the company. I have a sneaky suspicion he fancies her, too, but he'd never let that sway his judgement at work.

After a few more drinks and me bragging about the nameless women I took home last week, I want to know more about him and Jess. There's a spark in his eyes when he talks about her, and he honestly seems… happy. I've seen him happy, and this is a whole new level. His shoulders are relaxed, he's smiling more, and whatever she's done to him, I need the recipe. Gavin has another drink before telling me he's caught feelings. Not just little feelings, either.

"I honestly thought Sacha did a number on you. I didn't think you could feel this way. You seem completely smitten." I'm a pragmatic man, but I do believe in romance, and if you have something worth showing that side of you, you go all in. I'm not a poor, wounded man who has been hurt in the past. I'm a single child who had a standard upbringing, and nothing big or dramatic happened. I just don't have time for relationships. I wanted to get my career off the ground, and that's where I am now. Working with my best friend and enjoying life as a successful finance manager who loves his job and women of all shapes and sizes.

"I know it seems daft, considering how little I know about her personal life, but there's just something about her. I can't stop thinking about her." Gavin's eyes light up; he's definitely caught feelings.

We spend most of the afternoon and evening discussing the pros and cons of dating an employee, but in the end, I offer a gem of advice, "Being alone isn't making you happy, not really. If you think you can find something with Jess, then go for it. It appears that you can both still work well together, even after things have happened between you. Just don't break her heart. She's a good girl."

After a couple more hours of catching up, Gavin heads back to the office to finish a few bits before heading home for the weekend. A lovely redhead catches my attention at the bar, and with that, I strut over, not commenting on the eye-roll and smirk Gavin gives me before he leaves.

I notice this beautiful woman going back and forth between a table of men and the bar; one of them could be her boyfriend, so I tread carefully as I slide next to her, waiting for the barman's attention.

"Busy night for you fetching all these drinks." I smile at her, and she gives me a look that I can't place at the moment. Her eyebrows draw up for a second, and a look of worry etches on her face before her expression changes back to neutral, pleasant. It doesn't sit well with me for some reason, but again, I can't explain why.

"Yeah, my round, apparently." She offers me a sweet smile that doesn't reach her eyes and walks back over to the table with another couple of pints. The barman, Dave, comes over with my drink. We're in here often enough that I don't have to order.

"Does she look okay to you, mate?" I ask him, a feeling settling heavily in my gut. I'm no prince charming, but something is telling me to check on her.

"She's been on edge for the last hour. Her body language is screaming that she doesn't want to be here, but she insists she's okay when I ask." Dave has run this bar for eight years, and before that, he worked in plenty of pubs, clubs, and everything in between. There's something to be said for the psychology of being a barman; he can notice the slightest change in body language before a fight breaks out or if someone's upset and needs to stop drinking. He's great at reading people.

I decide to take a seat at the bar and watch the interactions between her and the others at the table. Dave's not the only one who can read body language. I notice the way her elbows are held tightly at her sides, and the arm that is not holding her drink is placed across her stomach. Although her posture is straight, she's watching everyone around her with widened eyes.

Someone is making her uncomfortable, and that's not okay.

Chapter Two

SOPHIE

My cheeks ache from fake smiling. These men are exhausting, and Richard is particularly slimy today. He's never been outright awful to my face, but I hear the comments he makes when he thinks I can't hear him. The team has been talking about the big projects they're working on, and I keep quiet about the smart house. It's something that doesn't get mentioned as they know how I got this project. I worked my ass off, but my drawings were ignored until the client accidentally saw them and was adamant they wanted them.

I've just got a round of drinks in, and there is a man at the bar who is cute and didn't make me feel on edge, but then again, my judgement around cute men is terrible. I don't realise I've zoned out of the current conversation and find myself checking the mystery man out. He's sitting at the bar, scrolling through his phone. Suddenly, he looks up and catches me looking at him, and I feel my cheeks blush at being caught and try to zone back into the conversation around the table.

"…so that's how I landed this project and gave her the best lay of her life." The men chuckle, and I roll my eyes. Josh is a dick; he was the intern with the Mickey Mouse drawings who got the senior architect role a year after me. He brags about sleeping with clients to get the jobs, which is unethical, but I don't feel I can bring it up. If he's willing to brag in front of the boss, then I know nothing will be done. There's only the owner above Richard, so Richard runs the show because the owner is never in the office. I've never met the man myself and couldn't even say what he looks like. His picture isn't on our website, and I couldn't find one when I applied for this company.

"Something to say about that, Sophie?" Shit, Josh caught the eye roll.

"Nope, nothing at all. You seem to be doing really well." I try to keep my face as neutral as possible and down the rest of my gin. "Anyone for another drink?" I say, standing.

"Trying to get us drunk, love?" Richard laughs, and they laugh along with him. I walk over to the bar and try to figure out a way to leave early. These pricks will be drinking all night long now. I step up to the same place at the bar I was before, and the cute man is still there.

"Back again so soon?" He quirks his eyebrow. He

has a schoolboy charm about him that makes me smile, a genuine one and not the fake, cheek-aching display I've plastered on all night.

"I couldn't resist clearly…"

He laughs and calls the barman over by name. How often does he drink here? "That's a nice smile you have. The one you've been showing those frat boys isn't your real one, is it?" So, he likes to read people. Interesting. Two can play at this game.

"Thank you, and no, it isn't. I can't stand any of them, but I work with them, and the one currently standing, throwing his arms about theatrically, is my boss. Therefore, I'm on my best behaviour. What has you sitting at a bar all alone? You seem like the kind of man who could walk up to any woman and take her home." The soft chuckle that seems to come straight from his chest is warm with amusement. It does something to me that I swore I wouldn't let happen again.

"That's where you have me, but I don't want any woman. I'm happy sitting and reading my reports this evening. People watching in a bar is much more interesting than sitting in my office." He nods to the barman, Dave apparently, who leaves my gin without taking payment.

"On me, love. You look like you could use an ally tonight." I raise my glass to his in thanks, and instead of heading back to the table where I really don't want to be, I stand and talk to this stranger, who feels warmer than those pricks over there, who are more like a swarm of wasps, ready to sting at the earliest opportunity.

"So, tell me about yourself, Red."

I roll my eyes, smirking into my glass, and regardless of the generic nickname, I give him an overview of me. The overview I created to tell people, the one that doesn't tell them anything too personal and definitely doesn't tell them about the person I used to be. He appears to be listening, like properly listening and not just nodding his head every few seconds. He asks questions about what I do and how I find the industry, and I give him my blanket answers, not my actual thoughts and feelings. You never know who you can trust or who's connected to who.

"That's enough about me, which is more than I've told anyone who hasn't even asked my name yet. I'm Sophie, by the way."

He holds out his hand, his face resting in a gentle smile. "Paul. Lovely to meet you, Sophie. Have you eaten?"

I cock my head at the question, noticing it's now gone seven in the evening, and I haven't eaten since breakfast. "Not yet, no."

"Well, let's ditch those losers and grab a bite to eat."

I smile at the prospect of leaving and, strangely, spending more time with Paul. I need to stop this; I don't know him, and the last man who had me smiling hurt me more than I ever thought possible. I'll stop it after dinner, though. A girl needs to eat, and he's my perfect chance to escape. Just as I start to relax, I feel a hand on my waist. I look around and see Richard is drunk, and then I notice the empty shot glasses on the table. My whole body tenses.

"Sophie, rather rude of you to be talking to someone else when you came here with me."

"Richard, the team came to the bar. I've been talking to an old friend I haven't seen in a few years." I look at Paul, internally pleading with him and hoping to high heaven that he plays along.

His expression, once charming, is now cold as stone as he glances from Richard's face and back to where his hand is. "Yes, Richard, and I suggest you take your hand off my friend." His voice is strong and almost protective.

Richard laughs at him and pulls me closer, causing me to topple off the stool I was perched on. "Richard!" I raise my voice, and Richard, previously drunk and cheery, has become scolding and angry.

"Remember your place, Sophie. I'm still your boss."

Paul stands, and as he does, Richard realises that he may have picked the wrong fight. Paul is broad and tall, and he's packing some serious muscle under that fancy suit of his.

"I'm going to tell you once, DICK. Leave her alone. You may be her boss, but in a social setting, you hold no precedence over who she spends time with. Now, you've had a few drinks, and Dave here is going to bring you and your friend some chips. I suggest you call it a night. It is a school night, after all." He nods at the barman, who wanders off into the back; I'm assuming to get said chips. Richard is silent and has removed his hand from me.

I take the opportunity to grab my bag and walk out with Paul. "See you in the morning, boss," I say not even looking back over my shoulder.

Chapter Three

PAUL

Well, that was a bit of a shock. Never have I ever made myself out to be a tough man. Don't get me wrong, I'll never see a woman being belittled or hurt, but other than holding a door open, I'm barely chivalrous. Something in me was on alert with Sophie, though. It took a while for her to appear relaxed; she was still wearing a mask, but she seemed comfortable. Until he came over, that is. She almost appeared afraid, and that's when I decided to play along with her story of being an old friend. I already wanted to take her to dinner, but now, I want to know more about her, which is ridiculous. I never remember a woman's name, let alone want to know more than what she does for work, and finding that out is more out of politeness than anything else.

We walk in silence down the road to a small Mexican restaurant. You can easily walk past it if you don't know it is there, but it's one I order from a lot whenever I'm working late. We sit at a table, and a waiter comes over to take our drink order as we browse the menu. Sophie orders a soft drink; I follow suit, not wanting a hangover in the morning. She hasn't muttered a word since we left the bar but is sitting with her back straight as her eyes flick between me and the menu.

"You okay?" I ask. I keep my voice soft and low since she looks like a deer in the headlights, and I don't want to startle her.

"Yeah, sorry. Miles away… Thanks for playing along earlier. I can't stand them. I have to work with them, and I've always avoided social events as they're misogynistic wankers."

I can't help but laugh at the way she describes her colleagues. "Please, do tell me more."

Sophie reels off a list of comments like how she's been passed over for promotions, continuously works harder than most, and is ninety per cent sure she's the lowest paid. I sit and listen. I can't account for the anger I'm currently feeling. I mean, we've just met, and I'm not sure whether we'll end up in bed together yet, but there's something about her that has my curiosity piqued.

Our conversation doesn't slow down when our food is brought, and we talk easily about how she's managed to get to where she is today, albeit a little slower than she expected. I honestly think her whole company needs a review of how they manage their staff, but that's not my place. Sophie looks a little lighter as she talks and eats; her shoulders are more relaxed and not scrunched up around her ears.

Her passion is evident in the twinkle in her eyes when she mentions the project she's working on and the ones she has in the pipeline and on the side in hopes a client will love them one day. I appreciate when a person has passion for their job, and she certainly has it. When the topic of conversation moves over to me, I talk about work, and that's about it, actually. Other than a handful of people I chat with, all I have is my work and Gavin as a real friend. I tell her she hit the nail on the head when she mentioned I was able to take any woman home. I don't mention it to brag, but I want her to know her assumptions are correct. I don't know why I want her to know that, though.

Time flies by as we talk and eat, and before I know it, we're walking out of the restaurant and need to go in different directions. For once, I'm not trying to get a woman to come home with me. A therapist would love to go through those reasons right now. I, on the other hand, ignore those thoughts and wish Sophie a safe trip home.

I'm now lying in bed, trying to understand what happened this evening. I saw a woman I wanted and had every intention of taking her home. But something in me stopped that train of thought. Instead, I felt protective of Sophie tonight. I mean, most men would have wanted to step in after the way her boss treated her, but after talking to her, it sounds like he's an absolute prick. I wanted to talk to her, get to know her, and that…that has never happened before.

As I toss and turn, I give up on trying to sleep and decide to open up one of my social accounts and see if she's on there. Nothing. I open another one. Diddly squat. I go through the apps I have, and there's no trace of Sophie Martin anywhere. I try my business social account, and there she is. One photo, very professional looking, a list of her qualifications, achievements, and some drawings she's produced and projects she's been a part of. Other than that, nada. There is no email address to reach out to her with. All I can do is message her through this app.

It suddenly occurs to me that this app alerts you when someone looks at your profile. *Shit!* I'm going to look like a right creep now, so instead of pretending that she won't get the notification, I send her a little message instead.

> Me: Hey Sophie, this looks like I'm stalking and honestly, I was curious to see if you were on social media. So, it technically is a little stalkerish… it was nice to get to know you tonight. I hope work isn't too bad tomorrow. Paul

It's late, so she probably won't reply. Feeling a little out of sorts, I get up and make a camomile tea to send me to sleep. I'll never admit to drinking this stuff, but it works like a charm. After a good twenty minutes, my head hits the pillow, and I'm out like a light.

When my alarm blares at me at six in the morning,

I shut it off and sit up to read through the daily news on my phone when a notification catches my eye. I open the app and read the incoming message.

> Sophie: It was nice getting to know you too, Paul. Today will be what it is. Hope you have a good one. Sophie.

Today is going to be a good day.

—

Chapter Four

SOPHIE

My body is shaking. I can feel it vibrating through my bones. My swollen eyes are closed tight, and I can feel the sweat pouring down my torso along with the bruising establishing on my ribs. I'm ninety per cent sure my head is bleeding this time. I can smell the dampness of the house; there's mould in here somewhere. I'm hoping it'll kill me before he does. Hearing his ragged breath has the hairs on my arms standing on end, goosebumps litter my skin as I curl up tighter into a ball. If I make myself small enough, will he forget about me? Can I disappear?

A shrill noise makes me jump. My body is stiff as a board, but I can open my eyes. They feel puffy but not swollen. As I take in my surroundings, my muscles begin to relax. I can smell my sheets, feel my soft pillows, and hear the sound of traffic. I'm not in that house anymore. I escaped, and he won't find me here. The shrill noise sounds again, and I realise it's the alarm on my phone. I reach over to turn it off when I notice a notification with Paul's name. If he tried to search for me on social media, he'd have discovered I'm not on there. When you try to disappear, you can't be posting photos online. The only reason I have this business one on LinkedIn is because I know he'll never look for it, and work insisted I have an account to connect with clients.

I smile at Paul's message and reply. Deciding how I woke up is not going to dictate my day, I jump in the shower and get ready for work. I note that my roots are starting to show if I look closely enough, and I quickly order another couple of boxes of dye for same-day delivery and head to work. Nothing is going to slow me down today.

WELL, THAT WAS A SACK OF SHIT. I CHUCK MY BAG ON the floor after receiving my parcel from the concierge. I get changed and dye my hair. Can't have anyone finding out I'm not a natural redhead, after all. As I stand in front of my bathroom mirror, applying my colour, I think about the positivity I had this morning, which disappeared quickly.

When I got to work, Richard was a prized dick, of course. He didn't like the show Paul put on last night and decided to take it out on me all day. He told me one of my client meetings had been cancelled, only for me to find out he took it himself, along with my drawings. I was then isolated all day. No one included me on the tea and coffee rounds. They all went out to lunch at the same time, which left me here to answer the phones and then sit on my own at lunch. To say I feel completely deflated is an understatement.

The dream of owning my own company is starting to feel like a joke. If these jerks won't accept me in their clique, how am I meant to employ and work with people like them? But I know I'm not ready; I don't know if I will ever be. If I can't get further in this company, I'll have to start again at another one, which is doable, but I'd rather not have to start all over again. Sometimes, it's better the devil you know, although I am currently looking through the senior architect roles available online. Sometimes, I like to kid myself that I'll make the leap to another company.

I chuck a meal in the microwave before I rinse the colour from my hair, and when I'm all refreshed, I slump on the sofa with something that does not resemble the picture on the box and flick through the television guide before settling on my comfort programme, *Suits*. As much as he can be annoying, Mr Litt makes me laugh, and let's not forget the inspiration for my hair colour choice, Miss Paulsen. After a few episodes, I drag my ass to bed and try to sleep off this dreadful day.

I wake up and feel as deflated as I did last night. Still, I get through the shower, put as much effort into my appearance as I normally do, and smile at my reflection in the mirror. Fake it until you make it, right?

I strut into work with my head held high and sit down at my desk. I notice no one returned my "Good morning," but I refuse to let it affect my mood today. After I've sifted through my emails, one of which was from my client yesterday wishing me a speedy recovery from the illness I apparently had, I look around the office and notice the shift in atmosphere from yesterday. Everyone has their heads down, their desks are tidier than normal, and most of them are wearing shirts rather than their normal polos. Mulling through these observations, I walk into the kitchen and make myself a coffee.

Standing by the coffee machine, Richard is with an older man I've not seen before, and Richard shoots me a quick glare as the older man turns to me and flashes me a smile that appears genuine. He's quite the silver fox, too.

"Good morning. You must be Sophie." He stretches out his hand for me to shake, which I do with a firm grip.

"Good morning. I appear to be at a disadvantage…"

He chuckles and looks at Richard. *Shit.* "I'm Benjamin Stevens. It's lovely to meet you."

I blush and instantly straighten my posture. "Apologies, Mr Stevens. I wasn't aware you were coming in today."

He offers me a kind smile—well, it is compared to the shitty ones I get from the rest of the men here. "No apologies needed; I like my anonymity. I'll be meeting with all my staff individually today to get to know you all, and I'll be coming into the office more often." With that, he nods to Richard, and they walk out into the main office. That explains the shirts. So they either got a heads up and I didn't, or they keep an emergency change of clothes here just in case they have last-minute meetings.

I grab my coffee, head back to my desk, and watch my colleagues enter the meeting room one by one. Everyone who comes out looks sweaty and a little paler than when they went in. Other than Richard, I'm the only one left to go in. Mr Stevens comes out of the meeting room and announces he's off to lunch and will continue his meetings this afternoon. I take the opportunity to head out and grab a coffee before my meeting later. If the others are anything to go by, it might not be pleasant. I try to enjoy my duck wrap and coffee, but my nerves are buzzing about this afternoon, and my mind is torturing me with questions. Will I be fired? Did Richard call him to get rid of me? What am I going to do?

I get back from lunch ten minutes early so I can have a minute to tidy up my emails before going into this meeting. I have a heavy pit in my stomach, and I'm sure I'm going to get fired. As I finish replying to my client, who I didn't see yesterday, Mr Stevens pops his head into the main office.

"Sophie dear, you ready?"

Oh God.

Chapter Five

PAUL

I'm currently going through the financials to send over to HR to add to the contract Gavin is signing off on. Jess's new role has already been written up, and I'm just finishing it off, but I still have Red on my mind. Normally, I'll meet a woman and maybe take her to dinner—although most of the time, it's just drinks—and we have a consensual one night together. That'll be it. But there's something I can't shake about her, and it's bugging the hell out of me. I haven't heard from her since the message exchange the other day.

As I finish up the task of Jess's new contract, I get a call from Gavin asking if I want to go for a break. I know his migraines are bad at the moment, and honestly, I could do with a break to distract myself from Red.

Walking up to the desk in front of his office, I see Jess squirrelling away, and I lean on her desk. "Congratulations on your promotion, Jess. Well deserved! I hear you're already taking your position seriously and forcing the boss to take a break. I can't believe admin hid you away for so long." I flash her a smile and go get Gavin for our walk.

We head out into the fresh air and walk towards our usual coffee cart.

"So, what's up?" I glance towards Gavin, who looks like the wheels are turning at such a speed in his head that it might pop off and roll on its own accord.

"The migraines are getting worse; Jess keeps bugging me about getting my eyes checked, so I've booked an appointment. I honestly think it's just stress, and you can't run a company without that." I hum in agreement, but other than Pierre and a couple of others, most of our clients are, thankfully, relatively easy to deal with.

Gavin fills me in on Jess taking the reins with Pierre, and I honestly can't wait to see what she comes back with. I tell him about Red, not that there's much to tell at the moment; I mean, I literally met the woman this week and nothing has happened between us, but she's on my mind, and this has never happened before. I have the feeling a one-night stand wouldn't going to stop her from living rent-free in my head.

Once we're back at the office, I sit down at my desk for all of five minutes before I'm called into Gavin's office. Jess has found some shady wording she's not happy with. We talk for a while before Jess informs us that she has a prior engagement, and we all know that means she's off to go out for a drink. We will pick this up again in the morning. Pierre is one of our European clients who, although he makes us money, is a slimy bugger when it comes to contracts. He'll try to sneak anything in, and he's trying to take more shares in our company than we are willing to give.

I finish up the day and head home. The tube is crammed with people, and, for some reason, it appears everyone forgot to wear deodorant today; I spend most of my journey breathing through my mouth. When I walk through my door, I change out of my suit into my tracksuit bottoms and a cotton t-shirt. My stomach is growling at me and aching, so I head over to the fridge and prepare dinner.

I've got the eggs on boil for my Tuna Niçoise Salad whilst I slide my phone off the countertop to message Sophie. She's been on my mind, and as much as I don't normally do second dates, or dating in general, she has the power to draw me in. I can't explain it. I feel different with her. It's almost like she's a Siren who cast a spell on me, to which I'll most likely be doomed, according to legend, but I still want to get to know her and explore this feeling more. As I settle down with dinner, I get a message.

> Sophie: Hey Paul, nice to hear from you. A drink sounds nice. Let me know when you're free.

Me: I'm free this week, give me a shout with what day is best and we can work out a place to meet that runs a low risk of your boss turning up.

Sophie: Lol that'd be great. Thursday, Duke of Edinburgh?

Me: It's a date.

After tidying up, I sit and scroll through Netflix, ignoring my tired eyes when my phone rings. Confused, I look at Gavin's name on the screen and answer. It must be important as he rarely rings in the evening.

"Hey, Gav…" I don't even get out his name before he's talking, and his voice is a mixture of worry, urgency, and efficiency.

"Paul! Sorry, mate, I haven't got much time. I'm on my way to the hospital. Jess has been attacked, and by the sounds of it, it sounds quite nasty. She obviously isn't going to be in tomorrow, and I'm not sure how long she'll be off. Can you please rearrange everything for the both of us for the next few days, inform HR, and field work calls until I know more? I know this is grunt work, and I wouldn't normally ask…"

"Go be with Jess. Update me as soon as you know what's happening. I've got it from here."

Gavin sighs with relief, thanks me, and hangs up. I grab my laptop and crack on with sorting through his requests as worry stirs through me. Jess is lovely, and no one has a bad word to say about her… I can't imagine why someone would attack her. I've come to think of her as a friend and not just a colleague; I mean, she is dating my best friend, after all.

After an hour of emails, rearranging meetings and clearing their calendars until the end of the week, I log off and trudge to bed utterly exhausted and drift off into a fitful sleep.

Chapter Six

SOPHIE

I sit opposite Mr Stevens, sweating from places I didn't know could sweat. Back of my knees? Check. In between my toes? Check. Pouring down the back of my neck, making me shiver slightly? Check. I must look like a bundle of nerves, twisting my fingers together on my lap as his expression softens a little before he speaks.

"Sophie, honestly, this is an informal meeting for me to get to know my staff. Please relax."

I'm still wound tighter than a spring. I feel like my emotions could bounce one way or the other. I offer a slight nod and try to relax my body, but it isn't working, although I do still my hands only for my toes to tap quietly in my shoes.

I can't stop thoughts of me being fired from storming through my head. I have to ask outright before I pass out from anxiety. Straightening my back, I poise myself in a confident manner. "Mr Stevens, am

I being fired?" The lines between his furrowed eyebrows distract me for a split second. Why does he look confused? Before I can focus on those lines anymore, they're gone as quickly as they arrived. His expression gentles again. "Apologies if I've offended you, I've been here a few years, and I haven't met you before. I just wondered if that was why you were here."

He chuckles, and I don't know whether I should be pleased or worried. "That's a fair point. I haven't met you before. If truth be told, I've been quite hands-off in my business for a good four years now. But that's all about to change. But no, Sophie, I'm not here to fire you. As I've said, I'd like to get to know you. Changes are coming, and I want to ensure my business has the right people for the vision I have for the future."

"Oh, am I allowed to ask what changes?" I seem to be feeling a lot more relaxed knowing that I'm not getting fired and apparently can't stop myself from being nosey.

"You're the first one to ask, my dear. I'm looking at streamlining. I've had an overview of the projects lately, and I'm not happy with the outlook. It appears some members of the team get more work than others." He raises one of those bushy eyebrows at me, almost as if he's silently challenging me. Will I spill the beans on what dicks work here? Or will I sit here like a good girl and let him think badly of me for that? Clearly, he has an idea of what's going on, so I don't treat him like an idiot.

"Mr Stevens…"

His hand lifts, and I blanch slightly. He cocks his

head to my response and lowers his hand. "Ben. Please call me Ben. Are you okay, Sophie?"

I feel my cheeks flush, embarrassed about my reaction. I'm normally so controlled. "Sorry, Ben. Yes, I'm absolutely fine." I offer him my practised relaxed smile, and we talk for the next hour, him asking questions and me answering honestly. I talk about my projects, the working environment, and all in between. By the end of the hour, I can honestly say I like Ben and am pleased he's going to be around more.

"May I ask what prompted you to come in? Like you said, it's been four years."

His eyebrows raise slightly, and his lips quirk up to the side in a humorous smirk. "Well, Sophie, when one of my friends calls to say the architect he's been working with for a while suddenly cancels on him with a 'sickness', and he doesn't believe it. Especially when her boss turns up for said meeting. My friend didn't gel well with Richard or his ideas." My shock must be plain on my face as he places his hand over mine. "Sophie, don't worry. It's not the first report I've had of Richard."

I feel close to tears. My client went to his friend, my boss's boss and the owner of the company, which is brand new information because he is concerned about me and my welfare at work. I feel myself sitting a little taller now, happy that my contributions are being noticed and are worthy of praise, something I've not had here before. As we walk out into the main office, we're smiling and laughing. It doesn't escape my attention that the whole office is watching this interaction. I mean, let's face it, they all came out sweating and looking concerned.

As I walk back to my desk, I hear Richard comment to one of the guys, "She probably gave him a blow job," and my newfound confidence comes crashing down around me. I don't let them see it, though. But I do clock Ben's eyes, which are now resembling the Hulk's right before he smashes. Apparently, I wasn't the only one who heard that comment.

"RICHARD!" Honest to God, I hide behind my laptop. I have never seen Richard look as scared as he does now. If he wasn't wearing black trousers, I wonder whether I would be able to see a stain.

Richard follows Ben into the meeting room, and it becomes deadly quiet. Crayons even offers to make me a drink. I haven't been involved in a tea round since that night at the pub. I wonder what Ben said to them all.

Chapter Seven

SOPHIE

I leave the office at five, and Richard is still in with Ben. I'd love to be a fly on the wall in that meeting. But I'm now in a lovely bath, my pasta bake is in the oven, and I can finally feel my muscles relaxing. I can't remember the last time my body felt relaxed; I try to think back to a time but realise I've probably been on edge since I left uni. The thought of that time has my whole body tensing in an almost painful way, so I shove those thoughts back into their little grey box and focus on the feeling of the water. It was so hot it sent tingles over my legs when I got into the bath. My breathing is becoming steady and rhythmic, like the sound of the ocean lapping at the sand on the shore. This is making my mind calm, and I can hear the bubbles popping, but what's that beeping?

Oh shit! The oven timer!

After I clamber out of the bath with all the grace of Bambi on ice, my pasta bake is successfully rescued from being a charcoal brick and devoured, and I'm now sitting on my sofa in the dark, worrying about work tomorrow. It's too early to go to sleep, but I also can't rest or watch TV because my brain is hyped up and whizzing through scenarios that are probably not likely to happen, such as Richard being in a foul mood, blaming me for spilling the beans about the work environment and Ben not being there to soften the blow, or it just being a normal workday and being ignored… and alone. My phone pings, distracting my trainwreck thoughts.

Paul…

My head stops its demoralising battering—like it wasn't currently spinning me into a mild panic attack. He wants to meet up, and I reply before my stupid brain tries to make this into some melodramatic scenario, too. Feeling a little better, I make myself a drink, grab the remote, and put *Suits* on to keep me distracted. Until bedtime, that is.

THURSDAY HAS COME AROUND SO QUICKLY. IT'S BEEN A strange couple of days, but Ben is "shadowing" the team again today. Richard has been quiet since his meeting, but I don't miss the glares that are occasionally fired my way. Ben sits down next to me with a cup of tea, which I graciously accept, and we start on what my day looks like and what I'm currently working on. This must be like teaching him to suck eggs since he's been in this industry for a long time, but he sits and listens, asks questions, and we fall into an easy rhythm as I work.

By lunchtime, Ben offers to take me to lunch. He's done this with a couple of others this week, but it's still a little shocking. I'm normally alone at lunchtime. We head over to the local café, where he pulls out my chair for me, and my stomach growls embarrassingly loud as I eye fuck the menu. I can see Ben's shoulders shaking whilst his face is hidden behind his menu.

After we've ordered our food—a chicken mayo and lettuce roll which has my mouth salivating—we fall into an easy conversation. Ben tells me about his wife and daughter, which I love listening to. It sounds like he has a lovely family. It's when he asks about mine that I stiffen.

"Um, my mum died before I left for university. It was a really hard time. My dad still struggles without her. My sister is the rock of the family. She supports Dad and is always on the end of the phone. Bless her."

Ben listens, offering a small smile and says he's sorry for my loss. "So, what about your love life? Anyone special?"

I can feel my eyes widening, my body filling with fear at the mention of my love life. I shove the reel of memories to one side and focus on Ben. He has wrinkles on his forehead and a whisp of a five o'clock shadow already forming, although it's only lunchtime. "There's no one. Well, actually..." My mind drifts to Paul and our drink date later today. He's someone who makes me smile and feel at ease even though I've only just met him. I realise I'm actually looking forward to tonight. "I've just met someone literally last week. But he seems like a good guy."

"If he isn't, dear, you let me know." He winks, and we talk about the business and exciting projects he has coming to the team. Just as our food arrives, my stomach makes another announcement to the entire city that I'm hungry.

We arrive back at the office, and although the last couple of days have been the same, I'm struggling with the heads-down and silent atmosphere in here. It's normally the lads chatting and occasionally getting their work done, but I suppose having the big boss around is a lot of pressure. For me, though, I normally just crack on, so having Ben around is quite a nice change. Ben and I have a productive afternoon, and he tells me about a project that would suit my skills, which I'm excited about. It shocks me when everyone starts packing up, and I notice the time. I start to close down my laptop when Ben nudges me.

"Have a good time tonight," he quietly says as he saunters away. The butterflies are currently attacking my stomach, and I'm actually feeling nervous.

It's just a drink. Not all men are like him…

Chapter Eight

PAUL

I haven't been to The Duke in years, but it hasn't changed one bit. It's lively and full of laughter, and people are concentrating on scribbling down songs because the weekly karaoke is starting. On the other side of the building, I can hear the clacking sound of the pool table being used. I got here a little early to secure a table for Sophie and me. Luckily, I was just in time because it's rammed tonight. As it's a nice day, I managed to secure one of the patio tables near a heater in case she gets cold later. I may not date, but I can still be a gentleman.

I sit with our drinks. I took the liberty of ordering her a gin and tonic like she had the night we met and then messaged Gavin to see how Jess was doing. She's home recovering now and apparently being a right pain in the ass, which makes me chuckle. I know her well enough to understand she'll want to be doing something, but she's on strict rest until she's given the all-clear. I look up to see Sophie walking towards me, and I notice she's scanning her surroundings; she doesn't seem like a nervous person, so I file that away to ask her about another time.

I stand as Sophie arrives at the table. She looks stunning this evening in a simple green dress that shows off her figure, her hair flowing around her shoulders.

"Hi." I place a hand on her shoulder and lean in to kiss her on the cheek.

"Hey, how are you?" she says as we take our seats.

"I hope you don't mind, but I ordered you a drink." My stomach is fluttering slightly. I know I'm not hungry. Why am I nervous? I'm definitely not going to look into that too deeply. It's just drinks, right?

We spend the next hour talking about work and general chit-chat. It becomes apparent that we're similar in a lot of ways. We both spend a lot of time working and have a very small circle around us by choice. I have my family, Gavin, his family, and now Jess. Sophie appears to have her family and some acquaintances. Talking to her one-on-one, I get the feeling she's guarded and not divulging the full story about a lot of things. Especially when I ask about university. She clammed up around this topic, and although everyone has a different experience, it sets a little alarm bell ringing in my head even though I'm unsure why.

I head up to the bar and order another round. Something in me is itching to find out about her past, but she clearly doesn't want to talk about it or is still trying to figure out whether I'm a serial killer, as we've only met a couple of times. After deciding to order us some chips to pick at, I head back to our table. As I walk up to her, I notice her back is ramrod straight and her hands are underneath the table in her lap, gripping her dress. She appears uncomfortable.

"There you go," I say, passing her a drink. She offers me a weak smile, and the tingles over my body are like a warning sign. "Are you okay?"

"Absolutely fine."

Nope, not having it. "Sophie, we've only met a few times, but you remember me watching you with those idiots you work with? That's the same smile you gave them. Do you want to go somewhere else or call it a night?" I don't want to go home yet, but I'm certainly not going to make her stay.

"Do you mind if we finish this and head somewhere a little quieter?" Her cheeks turn a cherry blossom pink as if she's embarrassed.

"Bottoms up." I offer her my most sincere smile and down half of my pint in one go. This makes her huff a little laugh as we finish our drinks. I motion for someone to take our table and tell them there will be chips on the way.

As we walk away from the pub, we talk about other places to go, but all seem to be quite busy. Thursday is the new Friday in London, after all.

"My place is only a few stops away," Sophie mentions quietly, her head whipping around in my direction. "But not like that. I mean…"

I place my hand gently on her arm. She seems

vulnerable tonight, and I have the feeling she doesn't go out often; however, I have nothing to go on other than the little bits I picked up tonight. If she feels safer at home, though, then that's where we'll go. "That sounds perfect." We jump on the tube and head over to hers. The minute we walk into Sophie's flat, she visibly relaxes. I didn't notice how high her shoulders were around her neck until she lowered them. Now, her posture is a little more relaxed rather than bolt upright.

"Are you okay, Sophie?" I ask as she pours us both a drink.

"Yeah, I'm just not great in busy spaces." I feel there's more to it, but I won't push her today. Maybe next time.

As Sophie prepares some chips—she apparently didn't miss it when I told the new occupants of our table there were some on the way—I look around her space. It's nice and tidy; everything seems to have its place. The one thing missing appears to be photos. When I scan around again, I don't see anything personal around at all.

I'm trying to think how to tactfully ask when she comes up beside me looking at a piece of art on her wall displaying a lovely seaside view.

"There are no photos about. They're all at my dad's house. I have a couple in my room, but otherwise, it's just this canvas I found of the Cardiff seaside. It was one of my places to go and think."

"It's beautiful. I bet it's even nicer in person. Do you ever go back?"

"No." Her tone is clipped, and my senses are telling

me that she had some form of bad experience in Cardiff going off this conversation and how she clammed up previously when we talked about university.

"Want to tell me about Cardiff?" I can't help the words falling out of my mouth; I really want to know what happened.

"Not today," is all she says before grabbing our chips. We spend the rest of the evening chatting about everything other than Cardiff.

Chapter Nine

I nearly told Paul, but no one knows that side of me. Other than *him*. Paul seems to like this version of me, and I'm starting to like Paul. He's so easy to be around. He didn't leave until nearly midnight last night, and it felt nice to talk and to have someone to talk to. I've not made friends, really, generally keeping to myself nowadays, but I forgot what it was like to socialise, talk about shit, and relax.

Paul noticed how I relaxed once we got back to mine. I think he's also twigged something isn't right with Cardiff. I can't mask my reactions; it's too visceral. I did elude that I'd tell him one day, and maybe I will. But I'm pushing that to the back of my mind as I walk into the office. It's Friday, and things have been a lot nicer around here with Ben's presence, although Richard has been uncharacteristically quiet.

After a couple of hours with my head down, I take a stretch to the kitchen for a snack and coffee break.

Richard is sitting at the table, staring into his coffee. He doesn't lift his head or acknowledge me when I walk in, but as I take a peek at his features, he looks more drawn than he did a couple of weeks ago, almost sad-looking. Most of me doesn't care—I shouldn't care —but there's that small part inside of me that hopes he's alright.

"You okay?" I say quietly.

Richard lifts his head, but he isn't scowling at me, which is a plus. "Not bad, Soph. Just having a break. It's been a bit of a tough week." He goes back to staring into his coffee, and I leave him be. As much as I hated being here when he was a dick, I also don't like seeing him like this. The vibe in the office is quieter. There isn't much banter there now, and although I'm more relaxed as I walk back to my desk, I notice the whole team seems a bit down.

I mull through my thoughts and decide to email Ben to see if he's available at lunch for a walk and chat. I'm not surprised when he replies in a few minutes that he is happy to join me.

Lunchtime rolls around quickly, and Ben swings by my desk with a smile on his face. "Ready to go, dear?"

"Absolutely." We walk out of the office and head to the little coffee shop down the road. It's a nice day, so we decide to eat our lunch on a bench opposite a little garden. As busy as London is, full of buildings and more popping up left, right, and centre, they are adding in more green spaces to enjoy, which makes my soul happy.

Stuffing my panini down my throat. I take a sip of

my iced tea and talk to Ben about the morale in the office. He's quiet as he finishes his wrap, leaning back to stretch his legs and take a sip of his coffee.

"Richard had a good old dressing down about how he treats people in the office. This is a business and not a frat house. Call me old-fashioned, but a quiet office seems to have provided a more productive work environment. And you seem much happier to be here." His bushy eyebrows raise at that last statement. It wasn't a question because I am happier to be at work now.

"You're right, there's no mistaking that. However, and I never thought I'd say this, I do miss the banter in the office, even though I was never part of it. It must be hard to balance keeping up a good morale and ensuring the work is done properly." I watch as a couple of black birds hop over the grass in front of me, chirping up every now and then.

"Where do you see yourself in the future, Sophie?"

I spin towards him at his question; I wasn't expecting this as a part of our chat. "Honestly? I want to own my own business, run my own team, and draw my visions for clients who come to me for my talents."

Ben tips his cup to me and gives me a wink. "Running a business isn't about trying to keep your staff in a cage. It's giving them the opportunities to build on their experiences, grow their talent, and fly to their next adventure. Richard is realising that in order for him to do that, he needs to change how he is at work. The team have had a similar, if not smaller, talking to. Your drawings are brilliant, and with some more work,

I can see you opening your own company. I fully support that and am here for any advice you'd like when you're ready." I stare at Ben, a little stunned that he just offered his help to branch out on my own. It's not often you find this kind of support at work.

We stand to leave, enjoying the rare sunshine on our walk back to the office. "And as for the morale, I agree. It has been a little down, which is why I'm going to be emailing out about a family BBQ at my house next weekend. You can all bring your partners and children. Come and eat, relax, and have a good time."

When we get back to the office, I feel much happier, and I do hope that the team comes along to this BBQ. It's personal opening up your house to people you don't know well. But I have a feeling this will be a turning point for our office.

When Ben sends his email, I text Paul to see if he's free to come with me. We're not partners, girl-friend/boyfriend, or whatever other labels there are out there, but we're friends, and I enjoy his company.

> Me: Hey, random question, you free next Saturday to come to a work BBQ at the big boss's house? X

> Paul: You asking me out on a date Red? X

The butterflies, which have no business fluttering in my stomach, rouse a small laugh from me.

Me: It's a strange first date, but sure
lol x

Paul: I'll be there x

50

Chapter Ten

PAUL

We arrive at the boss's house, and I'm not sure what I was expecting, but this looks to be a stunning house set far back from the road. A long gravel drive leads to a beautiful period property that I'd hazard a guess to say at least part of it is from the Tudor era. There's a sign that reads head straight round the back, so grabbing Sophie's hand, which I notice is clammy, we walk around the house.

"We'll leave when you want to. There's no pressure to stay." I squeeze her hand slightly, and she offers me a small smile, which goes with her posture. It's almost like she's trying to make herself as small as possible, not holding herself as she normally would. As we round the corner into the back garden, I notice a silver-haired man stand and start towards us. As he approaches, I feel Sophie relax her grip on my hand. I don't recognise him from the group she was with that night in the pub, so he must be the big boss.

"Sophie dear, I'm so pleased to see you. Some of the team is here already." He gestures to the garden whilst putting a hand on her shoulder. She releases my hand and pats his arm as he quietly says, "I honestly didn't expect many to come. This gives me more hope that we can turn the office around." He extends his hand to me. "Nice to meet you. You must be Paul. I'm Ben, the owner of the firm." He has a decent hand-shake, and I can sense his fondness for Sophie. She's relaxed around him, which is a good sign.

Hang on. I "must" be Paul? Does she talk about me at work? I shove my thoughts to one side as we go to grab a drink and mingle with other colleagues from her office.

It's been an hour since we arrived, and Sophie's posture has relaxed, which is great to see. I stand and listen to their ideas, projects, and how they want to start edging towards smart houses. They are even asking Sophie for advice because she's designed a few for clients already. Richard shows up two hours into the BBQ and seems much quieter than the last time I saw him. Soph told me about the grilling he got, which isn't a bad thing, in my opinion.

I step away from Sophie and the two guys she's talking to and go top up our drinks. Richard joins me at the drinks table, and I do the typical man thing and offer him a chin dip as a greeting. There's a moment where it looks as if there should be a buffering wheel above his head before he stretches his hand towards me.

"Nice to see you again…Paul, was it?" His palm is

slightly clammy. It's a warm day, but unless he's a sweaty person, I'd say it's more nerves.

"Yes, mate. Nice to see you, Richard. How have you been?"

We settle into a light conversation; he's actually an alright bloke if you take out his misogynistic traits that I saw the night I met him in the bar. He almost seems like a different person.

We're talking about trips we've taken in Thailand when Sophie strolls over, the corners of her mouth curving up. "Warming my drink for me?" she says with a light tone.

"Sorry, love, got chatting."

She takes her drink and wanders back to the group she's been talking to.

"She's a good one," Richard says, his gaze following her.

"She is. If you think she's good, why did you treat her like shit for years?" I arch an eyebrow, pretty sure I'm crossing a line here, but it needs to be mentioned.

"Honestly? I don't know. I've always been shit with talking to women. My dad was a prick, and I tried so hard to not be like him, and then I ended up being his double without even trying. It wasn't until Ben started coming into the office and held a massive mirror in front of me that I realised what a dick I was. I'm hoping to make it up to her."

I tip my drink towards him, and we clink glasses, nothing more to be said. I give him a nod and head over to mingle. I hear Sophie laughing; it sounds so natural, almost carefree, and it does something to me.

My insides tingle like a swarm of butterflies fighting over the last sunflower. Interesting.

The afternoon passes by in a flash. I've enjoyed spending time with Sophie's work family, and when it's time to go, Soph is full of smiles and seems happy. On the drive home, she talks fervently about the day, whipping her hands about as she goes. I noticed that even though it was busy at Ben's house, she didn't appear anxious like she did when we were in the pub. Maybe it's about the surroundings; I'm clutching at straws here because other than what she's told me about herself already, I really don't know much about Sophie, and when I try to dig for information, she clams up.

My mind races with what she could be hiding or even running from in her past. None of them are pretty thoughts, but I'm hoping one day she'll trust me enough to let me in.

Chapter Eleven

SOPHIE

It's been a couple of weeks since the BBQ at Ben's house, and honestly, the morale in the office has been much more vibrant compared to the dullness it was previously. We've moved the desks around so we're more of a horseshoe arrangement, able to bounce ideas off of each other and chat openly. It's what we've been missing, and I'm enjoying being a part of the team. I stood on the sidelines for years, watching their relationships grow, and now I feel like I'm one of them.

I've found that I enjoy the company of others, and maybe, just maybe, I believe I can have friends. It'll be nice to have something to do other than work and sit at home. I have Paul with our…whatever it is. Whatever we do have, it's nice. We enjoy each other's company; I am attracted to him, but I'm worried about catching feelings again. My previous carnival of red flags is not something I want to engage in again, and although

Paul has made no moves, I'm pretty sure he's attracted to me, too.

I'm helping Richard edit one of his designs. He wasn't completely happy with it and asked my opinion. First, wow! Second, our exchanges have changed, and the fact he's wanting or willing to ask for me input is a tremendous step for both of us. I'm halfway through when Richard pops a rose on my desk. I look up at him dumbfounded for a moment, probably resembling someone shocked with jump leads.

"Not from me, Soph." He huffs a laugh. "It's just arrived at reception. I'm assuming it's from Paul," he says, sauntering off back to his own desk.

I pick up the rose and immediately prick myself on a thorn. *Shit.* I suck the blood from the pad of my thumb and really take in the beauty of the red rose. Its petals are near on perfect, and the depth of the red reminds me of fresh blood. I'm not sure why, but I have a pit in my stomach. Trying to ignore that anxious feeling bubbling inside, I fire off a text to Paul to say thank you before getting back to Richard's drawing.

I've been so engrossed in this drawing, which is now completed and sent back to Richard, that I didn't realise it's gone two in the afternoon. I signal to the guys I'm off to grab something to eat and check my phone as I walk to the local coffee shop.

Paul: Hey love. Sorry but that's not from me. Who do I have to fight to keep your attention? ;)

What??

Paul didn't send the rose. There's that feeling in my

stomach again. It started off like a pit of an avocado, and it now feels like a bowling ball. No one sends me flowers. I walk into the coffee shop, food completely off the menu with how anxious I'm feeling. Coffee should make it all better. Once I receive my order from the end of the counter, I walk back to the office, mulling over who on earth would have sent me a rose.

I spend the next few hours going through emails, amending drawings for clients, and trying my best to ignore my anxiety. It's silly, isn't it? Women love receiving flowers, but from an unknown source, it gives creepy vibes. Ending my day feeling pleased with my work yet still anxious, I pack up my stuff and tell myself to relax. It's a rose; that's it. It's probably a kind gesture from somebody, and the card got mislaid. I start my journey home and listen to loud music on the way. It's one way to drown out the voices, anyway.

When I get home, Paul is waiting outside with the biggest bunch of flowers I've ever seen. I walk up to him and notice the goofy grin on his face.

"Can't be having someone showing me up, now can I?" He hands over the flowers, and I'm astounded by how heavy they are.

"Today must be my lucky day. Thank you. They're absolutely beautiful. Coming up?" He nods and follows me in. We didn't have any plans for this evening, but I'm not upset that he turned up. He makes me feel safe, and with how uneasy I'm feeling, this is exactly what I need.

When we get into my flat, I head into the kitchen to put the flowers in some water. They are stunning. I can't tell you what all the flowers are, but their colours are beautiful: yellows, whites, pinks, and purples. A sense of calm washes over me as I pretend I know what I'm doing when I'm arranging the flowers in a vase. Then I remember that I left the rose on my desk at the office, and it will likely shrivel by tomorrow. Oops.

Paul and I sit on my sofa, talking about our day and decide to order in as apparently beans on toast doesn't constitute a proper meal. As Paul orders our burritos, I go and change into something comfy with a stretchy waist because Mexican food always fills me up. I love that I feel comfortable enough around Paul that I can wear my leggings around him. We haven't known each other that long, but there's a connection that I can't quite describe.

By the time I walk back into the living room, Paul is flicking through a book he's pulled from my shelf. I don't have many physical books because I tend to read on my tablet, but he seems to be enjoying the thriller he's picked up. By the time dinner arrives, he's already a few chapters in. Honestly, it's nice having someone enjoy something I like, too.

When the food arrives, mine is practically inhaled before Paul is halfway through his. I didn't eat earlier, so I'm starving. That's my excuse, and I'm sticking to it.

"Did you figure out who sent you the rose?" Paul asks between bites. I shake my head whilst polishing off the chips.

"No idea. I'm sure it's all innocent, but something feels off. I have no idea what, though."

Paul assures me it'll be okay and that it's probably what I said earlier about the card being misplaced. The pit in my stomach returns when Paul leaves, and I can't fall asleep, so binge-watching rubbish TV seems to be my plan for the night.

Chapter Twelve

PAUL

"I don't know where to start. I've never been with a woman more than two nights tops, but there's something about her." I stare at Gavin, waiting for him to give me some sarcastic comment.

"But you haven't actually slept with her, kissed her…" His hand finds his chin like it often does in meetings when he's thinking about a proposal or an issue that needs fixing.

"No, nothing physical has happened. Would I like it to? Absolutely. But I just have this feeling I need to take things at her pace. There's something about her, Gav. It bloody sucks not knowing what's happening in her head."

We sit in our own heads for a moment. He's probably thinking about Jess; the lucky bastard literally had the love of his life right in front of him. Something that never bothered me. I am happy for him and Jess, and I didn't see that as something I needed or wanted in my life. Then in walks this redhead who, even though we're just... What? Friends? I feel like I want to spend more time with her, get to know her better, and maybe discard the fact I haven't thought about what our kids would look like. Who am I?

I decide then that I'm going to ask Sophie on a date. Not attending her boss' BBQ, rescuing her from her co-workers, or having dinner round hers. An actual date. In a restaurant. I ask Gavin for a recommendation for an Italian restaurant. I've eaten out plenty of times, but I haven't taken a girl on a date for... Yep, that's how long it's been. I can't even remember. Gavin gives me the details of an Italian restaurant that he likes, so I call and make a reservation for Thursday.

I leave Gavin to his work; Jess is in her office and waves as I stroll past. If things progress as I'd like them to with Sophie, I have a feeling those two will get on like a house on fire. Sitting back in my own office, I fire Soph a text.

Me: Plans for Thursday night?

She responds within a few minutes, which makes me smile.

Sophie: Apparently, I do now...

Me: Marco's Italian, 6pm. Thought we could have a drink after if you fancied?

Sophie: Are you asking me out on a date?

Me: If I were, what would you say?

Those three little dots appear and disappear for a few minutes. I've not looked away from my phone, feeling anxious to hear her response. After a couple more minutes of torture, she responds.

Sophie: Absolutely x

I'M STANDING OUTSIDE MARCO'S AT 5:50PM, PALMS A little sweaty, and my stomach is doing this weird flipping thing. I can't believe I'm feeling nervous; I haven't had this since my first interview many moons ago. I see her walking towards me in a dress that fits her curves perfectly. How she walks in those heels is beyond me, but her legs look magnificent. Sophie's hair is falling around her shoulders in loose curls, and the colour looks vibrant, almost on fire, with the light of the late summer evening. She is utterly stunning, and when her brown eyes meet mine, it feels like time slows down, and all I can hear is my heart beating. I feel as if I've been put under a spell, and honestly, I don't want to come out of it.

With a smile, she nears and kisses me on the cheek. Whereas I'm standing there, staring like a buffoon. Of all the ways I thought tonight might go, me with sweaty palms and not being able to move wasn't how I imagined it. However, we've only just started, so I still have time to improve on this odd situation I find myself in. I'm almost like a teenage boy taking out his first crush. Dear God, I hope that if it goes further tonight, I won't act like a teenager in that way!

I shake myself out of my stupor and guide Sophie into the restaurant. It is rustic and charming with a cosy, friendly atmosphere. We take a seat at a table lit with candlelight, and a friendly waitress comes to take our drink order whilst we look at the menu.

"This is a beautiful place. How did you find it? It's almost tucked away like a secret," Sophie asks, her eyes darting over the menu.

"A friend recommended it, and yeah, I must have walked past this place a dozen times before without noticing it. But clearly, it does very well." I gesture to the full tables of happy customers.

Sophie looks up just in time for our waitress to come back with our drinks. She's quite pretty but has nothing on the woman sitting in front of me.

"Hi, I'm Maria. Have you had a chance to look through the menu?" She offers a warm smile, and I've been so busy watching Sophie that I haven't glanced at the menu.

"Sorry, I've not even looked," I say at the same time as Sophie gives Maria her order,

"I'll take the chef's special lasagne with a side of garlic bread and some breaded mushrooms to start please." Maria writes it down and peers over at me with a polite smile.

"Make that two." I pass the menu and pick up my wine. It's not often I drink it, but I do enjoy a glass with my meal.

Maria wanders off to the kitchen with our order, and I try to pull my head out of my ass and make conversation with Sophie before she notices how nervous I am.

Chapter Thirteen

SOPHIE

I can't remember the last time I went on a date. It must have been before university when I met *him,* but it was more of drinks rather than dates. This is… nice. It's not that we haven't shared meals before, but it's nice to dress up rather than sit in my flat in my leggings, wolfing down a burrito. It's nice to be wearing a dress that I admit I bought for tonight. The guys at work complimented me this morning when I walked in, and they said Paul is a lucky guy. They assume we've been dating all along, and I don't know what it is we've been doing, but I can't wait to see where it goes. I'm not blind to his looks or charm. Have I fantasised about those lips on my body? Yes. Am I wary after *him?* Also, yes. But Paul isn't him. Paul is kind, charming—but not in a sleazy way—thoughtful, funny…and I am sitting here thinking about him as his lips are moving, and I realise I haven't been paying attention. Oops!

"…with Jess. But I wanted to let you know. You

okay, Soph?" He's looking at me over the brim of his wine glass. I have no idea what was said before, but I can answer the last question at least.

"Yeah, I'm all good. So that sounds interesting. Tell me more about it."

"I mean, I don't want to bore you, so I'll give you the highlighted version…" Aaannnddd, I'm saved. Thank God! Paul tells me about a French guy they work with who is trying to swindle them, and he's heading to Paris with Jess. Paris sounds amazing, and I know Jess is a friend. She's his best friend's girlfriend. A part of me felt a little jealous, which I have no right to feel. But as we go on, he tells me about Gavin's reaction to Paul taking his girlfriend away, and I can't help but giggle. I love their friendship and love for one another. I could easily let myself fall for a guy like Paul. Hell, I can feel myself catching something, and we've not even kissed. Something I aim to rectify before the night is over.

Maria slides our dishes onto the table with a practised flourish and asks if we'd like more wine. We order a bottle, and I'm hoping my mouth is containing the drool it's producing. This food smells utterly delicious, and there's nothing ladylike about the way I tuck into my meal. As I glance up to see if he's noticed me eating like I've been in prison for years, I notice Paul's eyes on my mouth as I lick the lasagne sauce off of my lips. The air suddenly feels thicker, and I gaze back down at my meal.

Why on earth am I nervous?

He's either imagining my lips doing something to

him, or I have a bigger splodge of sauce than I thought. Paul takes my pause to lean over and wipe away something from my bottom lip, his thumb soft but firm in its stroke, and it lingers a little longer than a "just friend" would. I pull in a shaky breath, and the butterflies in my stomach appear to be on some form of mission to bust out.

Paul finishes his lasagne and sips his wine. We've mainly eaten in silence, and he's eyeing me with an expression that I can only describe as if he were a lion, I would be a zebra about to be devoured. I gulp my own wine when Maria comes to clear our table and asks if we'd like dessert.

Patting my stomach, I say, "That was beautiful, thank you. But I couldn't fit a dessert in."

Paul shakes his head in a no and asks for the bill. "Still fancy a drink?" he says before downing the last of his wine. His elbows are on the table, hands joined, which he then rests his chin on.

"I don't mind. I could do with a walk after that meal, though." I'm looking for an excuse to spend more time with him alone. I enjoy his company, and tonight, something seems to be shifting. There's a charge between us. Don't get me wrong, he's always been attractive, but I didn't think he was interested in me that way. Tonight, though, I think I might have been wrong.

We pay the bill; well, Paul does after I argue that we should go Dutch, but he says with a cocky wink, "We're in an Italian restaurant, that'd just be rude." Leaving the restaurant, we walk. No particular destination in mind, but we gravitate towards the river. The sun is beginning to set, and there's a serene shine to the Thames tonight. Stopping to lean over the wall, I look down the river towards the city centre. It seems so quiet at night compared to the usual bustle of the day.

Paul stands at my side, turning his body towards me and tucking a stray strand of hair behind my ear, his fingers grazing my cheek slightly, leaving a tingling sensation that I lean into. The air around us thickens with unspoken words. The streetlight offers a softened glow around us as the sun sets further and the sky darkens. My heart sounds so loud in my ears I'm ninety per cent sure he can hear it, too. Paul's gaze flicks from my eyes to my lips and slowly moves back up again.

His hand is still resting behind my ear, fingers lightly stroking my neck, sending a shiver down my spine in a good way. I feel breathless as his hand slides to the back of my neck, slowly drawing me to him as he moves closer to me. I feel like we're in slow motion; he stares into my eyes, almost like he's asking permission to kiss me. My eyelids flutter shut as I close the distance between us, my lips brushing his lightly. The distant sounds of traffic are melting away as my body comes alive and moves on its own accord, my hands reaching behind his neck to pull myself closer to his body. His other hand moves down my back and holds me close as our lips part.

My heart is hammering, and I can feel myself breathing like I've run a marathon, and that was a small kiss. I open my eyes and immediately freeze. Did I do it wrong? His brow is furrowed, almost as if he's questioning what we just did. Shit. I shouldn't have kissed him. I try to back away, but his hands hold me firmer.

"I'm sorry. I sh…" I barely whisper as his mouth comes crashing down onto mine. The hand on my neck moves to the back of my head, holding me in place; he's in full control of this kiss, and my knees are threatening to buckle beneath me. He turns us slightly so my back is against the wall, and I feel alive. Electricity thrums through my body as my hands roam over his back and in his hair, and I grab the fabric of his shirt to pull him closer. His tongue teases my lips, and I open as if answering a command. My body knows what it wants, and it's Paul.

Our kiss feels frenzied as our mouths move against each other, tongues exploring, and I let slip a light moan as he nips my bottom lip. Still holding my head, he leans back a little, eyes roaming over my face. I'm not sure what he's looking for. My brain currently feels short-circuited and is struggling to catch up. He steps back and places his hand in mine. "Want to come back to mine for that drink?" We've not been to his place, only mine. The only response I can muster is a nod as I lick my bottom lip.

Chapter Fourteen

PAUL

I've kissed my fair share of women, but never have I ever felt that overwhelming, dizzying feeling. When she pulls back, I see the moment doubt flickers over her features. She tries to take a step back, but I can't let her go. She starts to apologise, but I crash my mouth onto hers, kissing her in a way that leaves no room for second-guessing or doubt. I've waited weeks to be able to kiss her, and to hell if I'm stopping now.

When I hear that little moan as I gently bite her bottom lip, I know I'm done for. I need to get her home soon; otherwise, we'll be arrested for indecent exposure. Mine is closer, and once I get the nod she wants to come back, I grab her hand and hail for a taxi. There's no way I'm waiting for a tube at this time of night.

Once we're in the taxi, we have fifteen long minutes until we're home. The air between us is thick with anticipation. The nerves from earlier this evening are coming back, and I notice out of the corner of my eye that Sophie is fiddling with the hem of her dress. That in itself is a distraction, so I take her hand in mine, my thumb running circles over the back of hers to calm the nerves. For which one of us, I don't know.

The city is still busy at night, with headlights and streetlights going by the closer we get. When we finally pull up outside mine, I pay the cabby and head up to my apartment. The silence between us stretches, and I'm starting to wonder if she's nervous, regretting this, or has changed her mind. I don't do sex without consent, and although I'm hoping she hasn't changed her mind, considering the chemistry we clearly have, I'll also happily make us a cuppa and talk the night away like we have done before if she has.

"Drink?" I nod to the kitchen, walking over to open the booze cupboard. I feel the heat of her body beside me before I actually see her. Sophie peers into the cupboard, leaning into me just a little. She doesn't flinch or move when I place my arm around her and grab her hip, moving her in front of me.

"Scotch, please." My eyebrows shoot up. Most women I know tend to stay away from that particular spirit. She looks over her shoulder and offers me a sly smile whilst reaching up in front of me to grab two glasses. My hand is still on her hip as her ass ever so slightly grazes my crotch. My teeth are going to bite through my lip if I have to hold this groan in any longer, although the twinkle in her brown eyes tells me she may be enjoying this little game. If it's a game she wants, then...well, game on, gorgeous.

She leans against my kitchen side as I go to the freezer for some ice. The glasses are sitting behind her, and her hands rest on the countertop with one of her legs slightly bent as her gaze wanders around my space. Closing the distance between us, the ice melting in my hands as I return to her, I stand in front of her, my arms looping around her sides to drop the ice in the glasses. I hear her breath hitch as I lean in and slightly graze her ear to watch where I put the ice. Pulling back a little, one hand finds its way to her hip as the other reaches for the bottle, my body leaning in closer to hers.

As I set the bottle on the worktop, she shifts to the side slightly, watching my every move. The pull between us is almost magnetic. My heart is threatening to break out of my chest with how hard it's banging against my rib cage. I want to taste her again, but only when she makes the move.

We take our glasses and walk over to the sofa. The TV stays off, and we just sit. She takes a sip of her scotch, and I find myself watching her throat as she swallows, her tongue gliding over her lip, and I notice her shoulders relaxing a touch more.

Before I realise it, I've already drunk the two fingers I poured and get up to pour another. I ask Sophie if she wants a top-up, and she shakes her head. Once I've poured my glass, I lean against the kitchen worktop and watch as she lets her gaze roam over the flat. There isn't much in here, just furniture and the odd picture scattered about. You don't tend to need much when it's just you.

I clear my throat, catching her attention. "We don't have to do anything, Soph. If it was a heat of the moment thing... I'm happy to sit and talk." I relax my muscles, wanting her to see I'm being truthful. I take a sip of my drink as she walks over to me before grabbing my glass and putting it on the side with hers. Her body is close to mine again, her hand lightly brushing my arm.

Tilting her head up, fixing me with a look that suggests she has all the power, which she does, she says, "Shut up, Paul, and kiss me."

Fuck! That's definitely a command I will obey. I loop my arms around her body, pull her in close, and crash my lips to hers with such urgency that even I'm surprised. I need to taste her; it's like she's my oxygen, and I can't breathe without her. Her hands are in my hair, tugging me closer. I move mine to underneath her ass and lift her up, the hem of her dress rising as she wraps her legs around me. I don't break the kiss as I stride to the bedroom with her in my arms. I'm so distracted by her kiss I don't notice I have made it here and nearly trip as my shins bump into the bed.

I lie us down on the bed and hover over Sophie, whose legs are still wrapped around my waist. Wasting no time, I brush her hair off her neck and kiss my way down from her ear, my nose grazing her skin along the way. I hover my lips over the delicate curve of her neck and linger for a moment before gently biting her skin. The gasp she gives me spurs me on as I continue kissing along her shoulder, trying to push the strap of her dress as I go. But this dress isn't budging. So, I sit up on my heels, pulling her with me, and unzip the dress from the back, letting my fingers glide over her skin as I go and unclasping her bra whilst I'm there before gently laying her back down.

My lips go back to peppering her with kisses as my hands slowly work the dress off of her shoulders and shimmy it down to her waist. As I busy myself with her dress, she flings her bra across the room, leaving the most spectacular breasts on display. I am definitely a breast man, and these are the perfect size for my greedy hands. Her areolas are a dark pink against her pale skin, with nipples standing at attention, begging to be licked.

Chapter Fifteen

SOPHIE

Paul is staring at me like a man who has been starving for too long, and I am the only thing that could satisfy him. I feel wanted, needed, and bloody sexy when he's looking at me like that. His hands gently cup my breasts as if he's trying them out for size. They fit in his hands, like they were made for him to play with. The sinful gleam in his eyes is all the warning I get before his mouth is on one, nipping, biting, licking, and sucking whilst his fingers tweak, pinch, and roll the other.

"Oh God…" is all I can pant as all of the electricity I felt earlier is shooting its way between my legs. He's barely touched me, and I feel like I'm close to coming. Paul is making an "mmm" sound that vibrates through me, and my fingers tangle in his hair as I breathe heavily. Paul's mouth is then on my stomach, kissing down as he yanks at my dress. I lift my hips so he can slide it off. A coolness reaches me when he raises himself off the bed to take my dress off completely. I'm now lying on his bed in my black lacy boy shorts and my heels. I'm so thankful I thought to tidy up down there before tonight. You know, just in case.

Paul slowly unbuttons his shirt as his eyes bounce all over my body, not settling on one place for too long before moving on.

"You want me to draw you a map?" I tease, not recognising the breathy voice that comes from me.

"Oh, darlin', I plan on drawing that map with my tongue." His voice deeper, sending all the sparks down to my clit, which is now begging like a hussy for him to put his fingers or tongue on. For someone my age, I've never had someone go down on me. The sudden thought that he might makes me nervous. What if I taste bad? Can I be bad at it if I'm just lying there?

Noticing the change in my body language, Paul kneels between my legs and braces himself on his hands either side of my head. "What's going through your mind, love?" His voice is full of concern but still sexy as hell.

"The thought of your tongue…I've not actually had…I mean…crap!" I throw my hands over my face, feeling my cheeks flame. Paul sits back on his heels, moving my hands from my face and pinning them above my head. My stomach flutters, and, my god, the way he's looking at me right now is making me melt before him.

"Are you saying that no one has tasted you before?" His left eyebrow arches, making him look a little like a young Sean Connery as I bite my lip and shake my head. I suddenly feel so inexperienced.

Paul grins and releases my wrists and smooths his hands over my body as his tongue licks between the valley of my breasts, down my stomach and even in the dip of my belly button before he reaches my underwear. "Then let me show you how good I can make you feel."

I feel my breath hitch as his eyes bore into mine, taking my underwear down with his teeth. Using his hands to take my boy shorts off, he then throws them somewhere across the bedroom. He picks up my right foot and starts planting feather-light kisses from ankle to thigh. My body trembles in anticipation, and he does the same to my right. By the time he reaches the apex of my thighs, I'm dripping wet.

Paul runs his finger through me, making my whole body racked with shivers. "Beautiful," he mumbles before widening my legs, his palms on my thighs as he dips his head. I hear his inhale before I feel his tongue run through my slit, making my body tense. Paul plants kisses everywhere and says, "Relax, love," as his hands stroke my legs. Before my traitorous brain has another moment to think, his tongue is on my clit and Fuck! Me! The noises coming from my mouth sound like I should be starring in a dodgy film on the internet.

Paul's grip on my thighs hardens so much that I'm sure I'll have bruises tomorrow. He licks me all the way down and then goes back to flicking his tongue over that sensitive bud. I'm trembling. I can feel an orgasm building, and, as if he's reading my body better than anyone else I've been with, he pushes a finger into me, curling it to find that delicious spot that I've only reached with a toy and was on the assumption men needed a detailed, step by step guide to find.

Fuck! I scream his name as the orgasm rips through me hard and fast. Paul's tongue and fingers don't stop until I've completely come down from the best orgasm of my life. He moves his body up mine, kissing his way up until he's resting between my legs. His blue eyes are sparkling like the ocean as the sun is rising, his lips curling up in a smug grin.

"Judging by the way you've just soaked my face, can I assume you enjoyed that?"

I'm still breathless. I feel like my bones have turned to jelly, and I want it all over again. I grip the sides of his face in my hands and tug his mouth to mine. Wrapping my legs around his waist, pulling him down onto me, reminding me he's still only half-dressed, I taste myself on his tongue. It's odd and bloody arousing.

Ripping my mouth from his, I demand, "God, yes. Now get undressed." I don't know where this confidence has come from, but as I lift myself up onto my elbows, I'm not hiding the way my eyes roam his body as he lifts his shirt over his head. Paul is toned, not overly toned like some of the guys in the gym, but I can see the outlines of his abs, and his arms look like they could throw me around without tiring. My tongue licks along my bottom lip, catching his attention. He watches the movement, his body still, but I can see the outline of what seems to be a sizable erection in his jeans.

He slowly unbuttons his jeans, and I swear this is taking hours rather than minutes. When he's finally undressed, I feel desperate for his touch. He kneels between my open legs, hovering over me with his hands on either side of my head, and a deep, intense look passes between us, piercing each other's souls. His lips meet mine in an unhurried kiss, one that has me melting against his bed, my arms and legs wrapped around him. A kiss that could make me catch something I swore I wouldn't again. But I fear it may be too late…

Chapter Sixteen

PAUL

"P-Paul…" Sophie whispers as I move my mouth down her neck. Reaching over to my bedside table, I pull out a condom from the drawer and roll it down my hard length. I hear her shoes clatter to the floor before I feel one leg wrap around my lower back, tugging me down to her.

Using my hand, I guide myself to her entrance, watching her face as I push the tip in. Fuck me, she's tight. As I push deeper in, her mouth forms a perfect "O" shape. She's so wet, and I can feel every clench of her pussy. When I'm fully seated inside of her, I hold for a moment, my dick twitching as her hooded eyes find mine.

"Paul, please move." Her husky voice sends a tremor down my spine as I retreat and slam into her. Sophie's back arches as a scream falls from that pretty mouth of hers. I am a tad ashamed of the fact my spine is tingling already, but this woman! I feel like my dick is in a vice, but this is no torture. I lift one of her legs, resting her ankle on my shoulder, pulling an animalistic noise from her, and my god, does it make me thrust harder.

I want to hear my name on her lips again. I can feel Sophie getting closer. I'm trying to list all the ingredients in my fridge to stop myself from coming, but the second I feel her pulsing around my cock, my name sounding like a strangled war cry, I'm done. I come so hard I can actually see spots. I fall forward, catching myself on my forearms so as to not crush this gorgeous being beneath me.

Never have I ever wanted a repeat, but I knew that this was going to be different. I'm also slightly concerned I'm never going to want to let her go, and that was before the universe-altering sex. Is it worrying I want to keep her after such a short time? Probably. Am I going to let that stop me from trying to keep her? Probably not. My brain must be short-circuiting because I can see Sophie's mouth moving, but I can't hear the words. Did I come so hard that I lost my hearing? All I have on a continuous loop in my head is Donkey from *Shrek* saying, "Let's do that again!"

"Paul, hey, are you there? Are you okay?" Her eyebrows crease in the middle, and she looks confused or worried. Shit! I'm more than likely crushing her. How long have I been in a daydream?

"Damn! Sorry, love," I mumble as I roll to one side. I busy myself with taking off the condom and tying off the end before tossing it in the bin next to my bed. Lying on my back, I pull her to me. I hate cuddling.

But Sophie feels soft and warm…comforting. It also doesn't take me long to note how perfectly she fits against my body.

"You still in cuckoo land?" I feel her smiling against my shoulder where she's laid her head.

"It's just been a minute. Sorry for crushing you." My brain is still trying to catch up with my heart, which is now beating contentedly inside my chest instead of trying to punch its way out.

"Since you had sex?" Sophie laughs, her breath making my smattering of chest hair move and tickle. "It can't have been that long, surely?"

The finger circling her shoulder stalls a moment before restarting. I don't blame her for thinking that. Honestly, I would have normally been with several women in the time I've known Sophie, but I haven't been with anyone since we've been…whatever this has been. I feel her fingers tap lightly against my stomach; it's like they're playing a tune. The movement is light, and I wouldn't notice it normally, but my body feels so in tune with her; I can even feel her heart beating at the same tempo as mine.

"I haven't had eyes for anyone but you, love. Not since the first time I laid eyes on you in the pub." I hear the sharp intake of breath. The tune she was playing with her fingers stops and thankfully restarts again after a few beats.

"Oh," is all I get in response. I suddenly feel foolish. Has she been seeing other people? And here I am, declaring I only have eyes for her. Rolling my eyes, I makc a move to sit up, but Sophie holds me down with her arm. I mean, if I wanted to move, I could. But I don't, not really. So, I settle back down and continue drawing circles on her shoulder.

It feels like minutes have passed before she speaks again, "You are the first person I've been with...well, actually spoken to since I moved here." Her voice is barely above a whisper.

"Did you move here years ago? After uni?" I feel her body tense against mine, so I move my hand down to hold her closer.

"Yes" is all the answer I'm getting for now. There's something about her past—uni, Cardiff—that she is hiding. It's something that makes her uncomfortable, possibly scared. I notice whenever I bring it up, Sophie shuts down, and I don't want that to happen today. I want her present and here with me. Therefore, I roll over onto my side and plant my lips on hers in a gentle, slow, exploratory kiss.

"Well, that makes me a very lucky man." And I mean it. My cock means it, too, because before I know it, I'm rolling on top of her and dry-humping her like a teenager.

IT'S BEEN THREE NIGHTS. THREE NIGHTS OF SOPHIE IN my bed...something I didn't think I wanted prior to meeting her, but so many things have changed in such a short amount of time. It's currently 02:22am; the time on my phone glares at me. I can't sleep, and I don't know why. I am enjoying this newfound cuddling, though. I didn't see the appeal before, but I can definitely get used to it. I'm just about to get up to make a drink when Sophie starts mumbling. She sounds alright tonight. I've not mentioned it to her, but she does talk in her sleep. It's only been a few nights; however, on the first night, it sounded like she was upset. I could never make out the words, but something about the tone was off. It woke me up, and I just stroked her hair until she settled again. The second night, she sounded scared. Like she was saying no, but the words couldn't come out of her mouth while asleep.

Tonight, she's shivering whilst whimpering. I pull the covers up and move to cuddle her. She clearly suffers from night terrors. I just hope they're nothing too scary for her. She's a tough cookie; I've known that for a while, but whatever she's running from still keeps her trapped during her sleep.

I turn to look at my phone, and it's 02:45am, I press play on my sleep playlist I use some nights and close my eyes. Sophie relaxes in my arms as the sound of the rain comes from my phone, and it lulls me into a semi peaceful sleep.

Chapter Seventeen

SOPHIE

I've got to go home.

Since Paul and I went on our date, we've barely left his place. We both worked from his on Friday which was good considering I didn't pack an overnight bag, and I just wore one of his shirts all day. Which was apparently quite distracting by the amount of time he spent between my legs instead of doing his work.

It's Sunday. I need a proper shower and some clean clothes. Although, I have to admit it's been nice being closed off from the world. With company for a change. I'm leaning against the worktop, holding my coffee, and watching the world from his window in a fresh shirt and some of Paul's boxers. I like his shower; I like wearing his clothes—possibly a little too much. But I do need to wash my hair now. It's starting to look utterly horrendous, and although he has lovely shampoo, he has zero conditioner, so my hair is currently resembling a rat's nest.

I hear the shower shut off and pour Paul his coffee. Is it strange how quickly I've become accustomed to being here? Yes. Is he dancing in a carnival waving a tonne of red flags? Not at all, and that is refreshing. It's the little things like he leaves his phone everywhere. He told me to go through his drawers to find something comfortable to wear. It's like has nothing to hide. Which is both lush and puts me a little on edge. Will the other shoe drop if I get comfortable? Knowing my luck, it probably will.

Paul meanders into the kitchen in nothing but boxers and a delicious, body-hugging t-shirt. I need to stop thinking about sex, otherwise, I'm never making it out of this apartment again. Just thinking about it makes me tremble with lust and anticipation rather than what I used to tremble with. That simple thought is like having a bucket of ice thrown over me.

"I'll have this and head home. Thanks for washing my clothes yesterday." I smile, although I can feel it's not reaching my eyes. Didn't I want to go home? Yes. I need my conditioner.

"How would you feel if I stayed at your place tonight? I have a meeting in the morning around the corner. It'd be nice if I didn't have to leave so early." My stupid heart skips a beat. I can see Paul studying me, almost as if he's gauging my reaction. And my reaction? Stupidly happy.

"Well, we can't have you leaving early now, can we?" I smirk. This time, I can feel my eyes crinkling in the corners.

It takes three hours for us to leave Paul's apartment. Mainly because I took off the shirt I was wearing only to have him pounce on me. Five orgasms and lunch later, we're finally at mine. I feel a little lost here now. It's only been a few days; this flat has always been my sanctuary. My safety net. But all of a sudden, I feel exposed. I liked being high up in Paul's place; it felt safer. I also know I'm being stupid. It's because I haven't slept in my own bed for a few nights, and even though they've lessened, the night terrors still give me restless nights.

Paul is in the fridge checking on what we can have for dinner. It's when he looks at me with a "what the actual fuck" face that I burst out laughing. I'm awful about stocking my fridge. If he's lucky, there may be an avocado in there that turned before I could use it. Maybe some out-of-date milk. I shop for what I need on the day. It's something a therapist would probably wet themselves over to talk about. I'm not silly; I'm almost ninety per cent sure it's because I'm still in flight mode and don't want to waste food or space in my luggage if I need to run. It's been a few years since I left Cardiff, and being in London will hopefully keep me camouflaged. Hopefully.

Paul walks over to me, snapping me out of my intrusive thoughts. "Right, you get your matted hair in the shower for some much-needed TLC." He winks and kisses my cheek before he starts to walk away. "I'm nipping down to the shop to put something in that expensive electricity drainer you have empty. You know the room with the big metal sink is for cooking in, right?" I hear his laugh as he picks up my keys and heads out the door.

Shaking my head, I walk into the bathroom to catch my reflection in the mirror. I look…I don't know. My skin is glowing, the black marks under my eyes have faded slightly, and other than my hair, which is currently in a messy bun, I think I look happy. It's been a long time since I've seen that dopey grin. The last time I did, it didn't end well. But…my stomach is only doing little flips for Paul…not trying to get my attention in a bad way.

Turning away from the strange but enjoyable view of my glowing reflection, I turn the shower on and step into the scalding water. My first thought is *yay to my coconut conditioner,* but immediately after that, I think *Paul's water pressure is better*. I laugh to myself whilst taming my locks. I feel happy. Not just the outer shell I put on for other people's benefit. I actually feel happy inside. It's probably the sex, but I'm sure it has something to do with the handsome individual who has been stroking my hair when I have my night terrors, who has been making me coffee with a smile, and who is happy to sit in silence without the need to fill it. Although I can't control my terrors, and I'm asleep—kind of—I can feel him comforting me.

The first night I stayed over at Paul's, I had a bad one. I should be used to them by now, but the feeling of dread and horror that fills me during them is something I'll never get used to. When I first started having them, I wanted them to stop, and at the same time, I wanted them to take me into the darkness so I didn't dread them each night. But this one, in particular, replayed a night I wanted to erase from my memory. One where I was having fun, dancing and drinking with my friends. Only to end the night covered in dirt, my tears leaving streaks on my face, flowing over the duct tape over my mouth. I'm sure one of my ribs had been cracked that night. I felt myself being pulled into the darkness, into the smell of mould and dampness. Then I felt him stroking my hair. It felt like a ray of sunshine breaking through the dense cloud and warming the tiny spot it shone on. That ray got bigger the longer he stroked, and I was finally free of the darkness. For that moment, anyway.

I take extra time in the shower, shaving my poor, neglected legs and then moisturising every inch of my body. By the time I finally emerge from the shower, I feel like a new woman. The foggy reflection still has her glow, but I can see the shadows in her eyes from the memories. Those eyes widen with fear when I notice the shadow behind me in the mirror.

Chapter Eighteen

SOPHIE

My heart is beating a thousand times faster than I'm sure is healthy. The shadow comes towards me, but I can't move. My feet are frozen to the spot like someone has cemented them in place whilst I am staring back at my reflection. My brain can't make sense of the situation. What was I doing before having a shower?

"Soph, you look like you've seen a ghost!" I feel Paul's hand around my waist. I'm still wearing a towel, and my body relaxes when my mind catches up, the buzz of adrenaline still coursing through my veins.

"Uh…I…I…"

Use your words, Sophie…and breathe. It's not him. It's Paul. Paul is safe.

"Sorry. My brain stopped for a moment. I didn't hear you come back in." I busy myself with towel drying my hair and chancing a glance up at his face through the mirror. Does he think I'm crazy? I can't read his facial expression. It's something I've grown rather good at; nine times out of ten, I can read what someone is feeling. Paul is unreadable at this moment. That makes me nervous. With his head cocked to one side, he stares back at me as if he's trying to read my thoughts.

"It must have been one hell of a shower. I was gone for forty-five minutes. And I clearly didn't do a good enough job of being memorable if you've forgotten me in that time." And there's the boyish charm. The sultry look currently on his face should be downright illegal. If I wasn't already in a state of undress, I'm almost certain my clothes would rip themselves off.

I lean my head back against his chest as he moves his body closer to mine. He still has one hand around my waist, and his other hand is stroking my cheek.

"Come, let's get you dressed and fed."

Now we're talking.

IT'S ONLY BEEN A COUPLE OF DAYS, BUT I FEEL LIKE I'M floating on my way home from work. The tube is stuffy; people are everywhere, but I know that Paul's coming over again tonight, and although it's still early, and I probably shouldn't want to spend all of my spare time with him, I don't care. I love it. I feel safe around him; the bags under my eyes are reducing because of decent sleep. I'm sure the multiple orgasms have nothing to do with it, and I feel lighter than I have in years. I feel so good that I decide to treat myself to a coffee on the way home from the station.

Waiting for my coffee, I scroll through my photo memories. It's not often I feel the urge, but there's always an old photo that'll catch my eye, reminding me of what I used to look like... before. When my name is called, I put my phone in my pocket, grab my iced latte, and stroll out the door. I notice a beautiful red petal on the floor outside of the shop. It's not until I'm walking back to my flat I notice that there are more. All the way to the front door of my building. The hairs on the back of my neck prickle, and I suddenly feel on edge. Shaking my head, I enter my building. It's in my head. I'm being paranoid and silly. Someone probably bought some flowers home and didn't realise that they'd dropped petals...in a line all the way from the coffee shop.

I hold my head up high, shoulders back, and feign the confidence I want to feel. There's that pit in my stomach again, but I'm going to ignore it. Paul will be here soon, and he'll probably laugh at me for over-thinking about the bloody petals. That's what I say to myself until I get to my door, and there's a petal-less rose stem on my mat. My heart stops, and I feel the colour drain from my face. Looking around the empty hallway, I see and hear nothing. There's only one other flat on the same floor as mine, and they're never in. I quickly unlock my door, go in, and slam it behind me, locking it and putting the chain in place. Leaning up against the wood that is cooling my hot back through my clothes, I scan around. Everything seems to be in place; it doesn't look like someone has been in here.

It takes me a moment to regulate my heartbeat. Am I being silly? I sink to the floor and sip my coffee, leaning against my door. I need to remind myself that I am safe. He can't find me. Not here. My mind strays back to a time when he wasn't so bad…

I'm tipsy, drinking whatever god-awful concoction this is out of a plastic cup. But this is university. This is how I'm meant to be doing it. Am I drinking my grief? Probably. But I'm going to enjoy myself and make friends.

It's the end-of-term party. Most people are heading home for a couple of weeks, but I'm going to stay, study, and look around Cardiff. It's meant to be a lovely place to visit, but I've barely left the university grounds. I throw the cup of crappy booze into a bin and head to the makeshift bar for a beer instead. You generally can't go wrong with a can of beer, right?

Just as I reach for a can of Bud, a giant hand grabs it instead. I'm about to argue with them until I take in the stocky, tall wall of muscle with muddy brown hair and eyes to match next to me. He smells delicious. I have no idea what the after-shave is, but it smells like bergamot and something woodsy. I realise I'm staring and quickly go to grab another can.

"Well, aren't you something?" He's only a few inches taller than me, but I still have to look up at him.

"Something? I'm not an object." I turn to walk away even though a tiny part of me wants more of his attention. I can't tell you why because he's said four words to me, but there is something about him that makes me want to both run to him and away from him.

"I'm Howard, by the way, and you're definitely not an

object. More like a prize." Howard is licking his full lips whilst opening his can. His brown eyes remind me of the rugby pitch after it's been raining. Deep, dark brown.

"Sophie, and I'm not something to be won either. Human being standing right here."

The rumble of his chest as he laughs keeps me rooted to the spot. He takes a sip of his beer, those eyes not leaving mine. I feel like I've been trapped by a tiger, and I'm not sad about it. I could do with someone like him throwing me about in the bedroom. It's been way too long.

Howard and I end up talking for hours about everything and nothing at the same time; his hand grazes my knee as we sit on the grassy hill near the party. There have been several other girls who came up to him and asked him to dance or grab a drink with them, but his attention hasn't left me at all. He hasn't been rude to them, quite charming, in fact, so they still walk away with a twinkle in their eyes. I wonder what makes me special.

My phone buzzes, and I realise it's nearly 3am. I stand up and say goodnight to Howard.

Brushing a stray hair behind my ear, he kisses my cheek. "Goodnight, Soph. See you around."

I walk back to my room…alone. Horny and already wanting to see him again.

Chapter Nineteen

PAUL

I'm heading to Paris tomorrow. Jess is practically vibrating with excitement, and although I'm looking forward to going, I wish I was taking Sophie. But then, I do have to remember that this is a business trip rather than a personal holiday.

Sophie and I have spent as much time together as possible. We feel closer, and if this is what a relationship feels like, I'm not sure why I've spent years avoiding them. It's easy with her even though she hasn't opened up about her night terrors or whatever happened in Cardiff. I have a feeling they're connected, but I know enough not to push. She closes down when I bring it up; she'll talk about it when she's ready.

I'll only be gone a couple of days, but I'm cooking us a nice dinner tonight. Who doesn't love a home-made Katsu curry, right? We're sleeping at Sophie's tonight; I've got my bags ready. I say bags, but I have one suit bag and an overnight one. She won't be home for a couple of hours, so I head over to hers and let myself in. Yes, I have the code for her building and know where her spare key is. Currently in my pocket. I couldn't believe she was leaving it out in the hall, granted it was hidden behind the skirting board. I didn't notice the cut line at first, but when I did, I was curious to see what it was. Lo and behold, some of the plaster had been carefully removed to provide a neat hiding place for her spare key.

As I'm pottering about in the kitchen, I spot a flower stem in the rubbish bin. Odd. She got that rose weeks ago at work, and I'm sure she left it there. Thinking nothing more of it, I crack on with my dicing and simmering. I open the bottle of wine and pour two glasses, knowing she'll be home any minute. As if on demand from my thoughts, the lock turns, and the door opens. Sophie is a beautiful woman; her brown eyes shimmer in the low light of her doorway. As she nears the kitchen, I can see a smidge of roots showing. I've guessed Sophie isn't a natural redhead for a couple of weeks. I also haven't let on that I know. I'm not stupid. She clearly puts in a lot of effort covering her natural colour, but from the tiny spec I've seen, it could possibly be blonde. Blonde would suit her, I think.

Quickly tearing my eyes away before she notices, I give her a peck on the cheek and hand her wine over.

"I could get used to this service, you know." Her eyes are sparkling with humour as she takes a sip and kicks off her shoes.

I flash her my usual charming smile as I head back

to the hob to stir the sauce. After dishing it up, I take our plates over to where she's sat on the sofa. She's already bought over my wine and cluttery.

"So, Ben's going to be in the office for a few days?" I remember her mentioning it but couldn't remember when he was coming. I know she enjoys spending time with him at work.

"Yeah, he'll be there tomorrow for a couple of days before he has some time off. Apparently, even the boss needs annual leave." When she pops a piece of chicken into her mouth, she makes this humming sound that shoots straight to my cock, and now all I can think about is her humming around it. However, what it looks like is me getting a hard-on whilst talking about her boss. I move my bowl over my lap to better cover myself as Sophie talks through her work plans for the next couple of days whilst Ben is in the office.

We finish dinner, which is utterly delicious, if I do say so myself, and take our dishes to the kitchen. Sophie is leaning over to load the dishwasher and the way her skirt hugs her ass… Well damn! When she straightens, I prowl over, and her eyes widen. There's a hint of challenge in the way she straightens her spine and places her hands on the countertop behind her.

I move my body in front of hers, hands to the side of hers, pinning her in. "Do you know what you do to me?" The breath is knocked out of me when her leg hooks around the back of mine to bring me closer.

"Not got a clue." Her breathless chuckle is all I get before her hands wrap around the back of my neck and bring my lips crashing to hers.

Wasn't I going to do this to her? Why am I even in my head right now?

Bringing myself back into the moment, I grab her hips and hoist her onto the countertop. Sophie's legs lock around me, keeping us intertwined in a never-ending kiss. I taste the sweetness of the curry as my tongue strokes hers. Even that is turning me on. This woman tastes like my cooking. She tastes like mine.

Interesting. Mine?

Without taking my lips from hers, I pick her up and carry her towards the bedroom. I'm going to need my fill tonight; I've gotten too used to being with her, and I'm going to miss the hell out of her whilst I'm away.

Lowering us down onto the bed, Sophie's legs are still firmly wrapped around me. Her skirt has shifted up around her waist, and I slide my hands from around her waist up to her thigh. She has wonderfully firm, thick thighs that I intend to spend a long time memorising. I lean back to catch my breath from our kiss, just in time to notice how her skin pebbles with goose-bumps as my hand glides across her smooth skin. As I reach the curve of her ass, I firmly squeeze. Damn, her ass is fine. I could touch her all day and never be bored. As much as I love the physical reaction from my touch, it's her facial expression that calls my attention.

Her lips, swollen and a darker pink from our kiss, are parted slightly; her eyes burn with a dark, smouldering hunger, and her pupils are blown wide with desire. The heat radiating from her gaze, tracing over every inch of my face and down my body, calls to me on a primal level. Leaning into her, I feel Sophie's breath quicken further as my lips locate the pulse spot on her neck. I nibble and suck lightly, biting a little harder as a moan slips from her mouth. Trailing kisses down her neck, my hands make fast work of the buttons on her blouse, exposing her soft breasts.

I kiss her skin across her collarbone and through the valley of her breasts. Feeling her hands fumble with my trousers, I give her a helping hand by undoing my belt and trousers, shoving them down as I lick my way over her soft, supple skin to the waist of her skirt. I'm assuming the zip is one of those hidden ones which are incredibly annoying in moments like this, so I don't waste time trying to locate it. I leave her skirt on and drag down her black lace thong and throw it behind me, taking her ankles and pulling her to the edge of the bed as I lower to my knees.

"I need my dessert," is all the warning I give her before my tongue runs through her. She is dripping for me already, and fuck me if she doesn't taste sweet tonight. Sophie is trembling under my hands as I hold her thighs apart, tongue circling her clit and teasing her entrance with my finger.

"Fuck, Paul, I swear to G…" Sophie's words are swapped for a guttural moan as I push my finger into her, swirling it around. Feeling her squeeze me, I increase the firmness as I circle her clit and add another finger to her tight pussy, already feeling her orgasm building. It's not long before Sophie's fingers are pulling my hair, and she's riding my face through her orgasm. Feeling her come around my fingers and on my tongue is becoming one of my favourite things.

I smugly lean back on my heels, running my tongue over my lips, tasting her whilst watching her chest rise and fall as she tries to regulate her breathing. When Sophie rises up on her elbows, she stares at me through hooded eyes, and her pupils so wide they turn her brown eyes almost black. Licking her lips, she slides off the bed onto my lap and kisses me. She hums, savouring her own flavour, spreading her arousal on my throbbing cock. Sophie positions herself and slams down, bringing a groan from the depths of my soul. Rocking her hips in a way that makes me feel every part of her has me nearly blowing there and then. I make a mental note of all the emails I need to respond to at work just to keep my mind off of the fact this goddess is riding me like her life depended on it.

My hands grip her hips, guiding her rhythm, but Sophie isn't having it. She plants her hands on my chest and takes control, grinding down with a slow, torturous roll of her hips that has my vision going white at the edges.

"Jesus, Sophie," I growl, head tipping back.

Her breathy laugh is pure sin. "Losing control already?"

I dig my fingers into her thighs in retaliation, shifting my hips up to meet hers with enough force to make her cry out. Her nails bite into my shoulders, and I can feel the tremble in her body as she starts to tighten around me.

"Paul…" My name is half a plea, half a curse, and when she finally lets go, her body shuddering around me, I follow her over the edge with a deep, guttural groan tearing from my throat as pleasure crashes through me.

For a moment, neither of us moves. The only sound is our heavy breathing. Our slick skin has melded together as we come down. Sophie slumps forward, pressing her forehead to mine, and I brush the damp hair from her face.

"I'm gonna miss this," I murmur, voice rough with lingering pleasure.

Sophie lets out a soft chuckle, fingers tracing idle patterns across my chest. "You'll miss me, you mean. It's only for a couple of days."

I tip her chin up, making her meet my gaze. "Yeah. You. Days."

Something flickers in her expression, something softer beneath all the heat and desire. She doesn't say anything, just leans in and kisses me—slow this time, lingering, like she's memorising me as much as I'm memorising her.

And fuck, if that doesn't undo me more than anything else.

Chapter Twenty

SOPHIE

Three new clients, two projects closing, and a general meeting today. At least, I get to see Ben and have a coffee lunch with him. I like spending time with Ben because he reminds me of my dad. Well, before my mum died. He's a shell of the man he used to be now, but grief takes us all differently.

I'll always carry some guilt in leaving him and my sister after Mum died. I'd already secured my place at uni and didn't want to delay a year. Did I run away and avoid my grief? Probably. Did that lead to some dark times? Absolutely.

Shaun Taylor was a man of few words, but he adored my mum, Betty, more than anything in the world. Their love story is one my sister Coral and I used to aspire for. They met at a concert in a pub. Their eyes met across a crowded, smoke-filled room— because this was back in the days when you could smoke everywhere—and he bought her a lager and lime. He wooed her, took her to see another local band, dinner, drinks, flowers... After only three months, he dropped down on one knee and proposed. He'd met the love of his life, and she'd met hers.

They married in the local church, surrounded by their friends and family, which turned out to be the majority of the village they lived in. Nine months later, Coral arrived in the world. Their first daughter. My parents always told us it felt like their hearts expanded so much they needed another daughter to fill the space that was meant for all this love. Two years later, I came into the world, and our family was complete.

We weren't a rich family, nor were we poor. We had everything we needed and treats along the way. The happiest childhood I could imagine, and honestly, I would never change my parents or sister. The only thing I would change is when I was 16, my mum felt a little off. That trip to the doctors and the follow-ups after that felt like our little bubble was going to burst. Breast cancer can fucking suck it. It took one of the most loving, amazing women I knew from us the summer before I was set to move to Cardiff.

I can't explain the pain of losing a parent. All I know is that a part of me died with her that day, and when I went to Cardiff, even more of me died by the time I'd finished my five years. I was no longer Sophie Taylor. It was Sophie Taylor who escaped and made her way to London, but it was Sophie Martin who emerged. A shell of her former self, protected and adamant that she was never going to let another man into her broken heart ever again.

Until Paul.

I pop a reminder on my phone to call home tonight. It's been a few months, and Paul isn't back until tomorrow, so I will Facetime and let my dad tell me how he hates my hair colour; he prefers it natural like Coral's. I feel a sad smile touch my lips as Ben approaches my desk and pulls me out of my thoughts.

"Sophie, my dear. Ready for coffee?" His eyes are bright. From the day I first met Ben and thought he was going to fire me, it's his eyes that have always caught my attention.

"Absolutely!" I beam up at him.

We head over to our usual coffee place and sit on our bench since it's such a beautiful day. Ben always insists on paying for lunch; I'm not complaining, though. London is bloody expensive!

Ben sits next to me, handing me my latte and a filled croissant, which I immediately start shovelling into my face. I didn't realise how hungry I was until now.

"Tell me, Sophie, how's this man of yours?" He laughs as I choke on my food.

After swallowing what feels like lumpy air, I answer him, "Mine? We haven't really…I mean…I don't think we're an item?"

Are we an item? We haven't labelled anything. Is he my man?

"Oh, Sophie, he's definitely yours. The man practically has love hearts in his eyes when he looks at you. And the way you look at him?" Ben's head is cocked to one side, his lips tilted up, and one annoying "I told you so" eyebrow raised as the dawn of realisation hits me like a freight train.

We may not have said it to each other, but as far as I'm aware, neither of us is seeing anyone else. We spend almost every night together and have spent the last couple of weekends in each other's company, too. Shit! When did I get into a relationship? I sit for a moment, sipping my latte, which I now realise is still too hot, and I've burnt my tongue. I'm not panicking. I honestly thought my last relationship put me off for life, but Paul is so easy to be with. He's calm and kind and doesn't push when he clearly knows something went on in Cardiff; I can see those cogs turning in his brain when I sidestep the subject. He's amazing in bed, generous, and makes me feel…well, he makes me feel.

Ben is leaning back, devouring his own croissant, which appears to be loaded with mozzarella with how stringy the cheese looks, appearing rather smug.

"Well, shit. You've got me there. I suppose he is my man. And he's perfect. In Paris actually with his colleague Jess." Ben turns abruptly with a shocked expression lining his features. Letting out a small giggle, I say, "Oh, nothing to worry about there. Jess is his best friend's girlfriend. They all work together, and as much as he adores her, it is definitely platonic. Almost brotherly. It's sweet. Apparently, we're going on a double date soon, so I get to meet them."

I let that sit with Ben whilst I take advantage of the silence and shovel the last of my croissant into my mouth before I die of starvation. When I'm finally satisfied, Ben pulls out a couple of KitKats from his pocket. Honestly, this man is going to make an amazing grandad with magic pockets like this. And as if by magic, he goes on to tell me about how his daughter is pregnant, and he cannot wait to be the doting grandad. We talk for a while about Paul and me and what Ben's planning to build in his garden for what sounds like an army of grandkids.

Chapter Twenty-One

PAUL

I am so proud of how Jess handled Pierre this week. She has a talent for this, and Gavin was a hundred per cent right in promoting her. Her concussion, other than giving her time off and obviously pain, hasn't hindered her eye for detail at all. After my debrief with Gavin, I head home to drop my bags off, shower, and change before heading over to Sophie's.

I bought her a necklace whilst on my trip. As I stand in my towel looking at the open box on the bed, I'm doubting myself. Is it too early to buy jewellery? We haven't labelled what we are, but I haven't looked twice at another woman since meeting Sophie for the first time that night in the pub. Will she like it?

It's a simple, delicate silver chain with a dainty silver heart and a single diamond in it. When Jess and I went shopping, I didn't know what I wanted to get; I just knew I wanted to get Sophie something. I was drawn to this necklace, and when we got back to the hotel, Jess told me she thought it symbolised my affection for Sophie. Simple, yet meaningful. She got all up in my head, and even though I felt like I was catching feelings before, I have this grounding feeling now. Knowing that there is no one like her, it's as if Sophie is meant to be mine. But, in case she feels differently—which may crush not only my ego but my bloody heart that seems to have caught big feelings—this is simply a friendly necklace.

By the time I get my arse in gear and get to Sophie's, she's already in and pottering about her flat. I let myself in and walk up behind her as she's folding washing.

"Oh my GOD, Paul! You scared the shit out of me!" She's loud, but she spins around and hugs me like we haven't seen each other in months.

"Hello to you too, darlin'." I seal my lips over hers, needing to feel more of her on me. This can't just be me making this up, right? This kiss *feels* like it has meaning. More than friends, more than friends with benefits.

It feels like she is mine.

The thought hits me hard right in my chest. Right in my gut. It's not a passing feeling; it's a deep, instinctual knowing. Like something ancient and primal waking up inside me. I want to mark her, claim her, and make sure she understands exactly what she means to me. Not in some caveman-dragging-his-woman-by-the-hair way, but in a way that leaves no doubt. Sophie is it for me.

I force myself to step back, even though every muscle in my body is screaming at me to stay pressed up against her. It's like my body is wired to hers, and the second there's space, something inside me becomes tense and restless.

By the time I pull the box from my bag, my palms are damp. Sweaty? What the hell? I don't get nervous. But this? This matters. It's not just a necklace. It's me putting my heart in her hands and hoping she doesn't crush it.

When she gasps at the sight of the box, my chest swells. It's not just pride. It's something deeper, older. A need to provide. To give. To see her wear something I chose for her and know, in some small way, she's carrying a piece of me.

As I clasp the necklace around her neck, my fingers brush her skin, and I swear I feel a shiver run through her. Her hand immediately rises to touch the heart. My heart. I swallow hard, trying to keep my voice steady when I say, "It looks good on you, love." The therapist in my head would probably call it my inner caveman coming out. Maybe they're right. But I don't care. All I know is that Sophie is mine.

And I'll spend the rest of my life making sure she knows it.

Sophie takes a moment to look at her reflection in the window, and her eyes find mine without turning around. We share a moment, simply staring at each other through the window's vision of us. If anyone actually looks into her window from the block across the street, they will probably think we're a pair of weirdos or something.

But at this moment, I'd take any label, any game. This woman is mine, and I'm fairly certain she's feeling it, too. Sophie's body turns back to mine, our gazes finding each other's again, and there's a spark, an electrical current passing through us. Not just lust. It's almost like there's a new form of connection.

"Paul, I absolutely love it." Sophie's voice is quiet but firm. I take the few steps separating us to reach her, and my hands cup her face as I kiss her slowly, almost like I'm claiming her. Her hands reach my shoulders, holding on as we embrace.

"Love, as much as I want to kiss you all night, I need to eat dinner."

She snorts a laugh as she grabs her phone from the kitchen counter. "What you fancying?" she says absent-mindedly whilst opening a delivery app on her phone.

"Anything you want as long as I get to have you for dessert." I grab her waist and pull her to me, causing her to shriek as I scroll through the app and pick a restaurant at random.

Dinner arrives in thirty minutes—the joys of living in the city—and we catch up on the last few days as we devour our Singapore noodles. Sophie lights up as she tells me about her new clients and listens intently as I tell her about Jess's bad-assery in Paris.

"I'd love to go to Paris," she says, sighing into her noodles after listening to me talk about the city.

"Luckily for you, I don't intend on leaving you

behind next time," I say, winking at her. The smile that hits me is brighter than the sun. That settles it in my mind. We're in a relationship, even if we haven't said it out loud.

Chapter Twenty-Two

SOPHIE

With a rare afternoon off work, I decided to take myself shopping. I need some new clothes and want to treat Paul…and myself to some new underwear. My hand touches the necklace he bought me. It's such a beautiful gift, making my heart warm when I think about it. I think the last time someone bought me jewellery was for my sixteenth birthday. My mum and dad bought me a bracelet. It's tucked safely in my jewellery box. I'd wear it more often, but back then, the trend was big and chunky. It has a big 16 dangling from it and isn't really my style anymore. But I keep it for the treasured memories.

Latte in hand, I wander around, trying to remember what underwear stores look like. I normally shop online, but I wanted to come out of my comfort zone and actually try some on before I buy. I should probably get measured, too. I haven't been properly measured since my twenties. Heading into a shop, I browse the countless bras and different underwear sets. Clearly looking like I need help, I see a sales assistant make her way over to me.

"Good afternoon. Is there anything I can help you with today?" The girl has a wide customer service smile, and her brown hair hangs straight past her shoulders.

"Hi. Yes, actually. I could probably do with being measured and possibly help choosing some pieces?" I can feel the nerves radiating off of me. Shopping isn't my greatest strength, and handing control over to someone, no matter how small, still feels a little scary. Unless it's Paul apparently. His presence makes me feel comfortable and at ease.

"Absolutely. My name's Masie. Please follow me, and we'll get you set up." She starts walking to the back of the store, where I can only assume the changing rooms are.

"Nice to meet you, Masie. I'm Sophie." I touch the necklace again, almost like I'm drawing comfort from him through it, whilst following Masie.

Once I've stripped off my top and downed the last of my latte, Masie is with me, talking through measurements and different styles that will suit my body. When she's gotten the numbers she needs, she scampers off to the shop floor to pick me up some items. I stand there, staring at my reflection. The bra I'm wearing is off-white—it used to be white—and a little frayed at the edges now that I look closer. When did I buy this? It's super comfy, though, so I probably won't bin yet.

As I hear footsteps walking back to the changing

room, I feel prickles on my neck. The kind I used to have when I was in Cardiff, not the new kind Paul is making my body create. Feeling slightly on edge, I jump back into the mirror when Maisey speaks asking if it's okay to come in.

"Sophie, are you okay? You look like you've seen a ghost." The concern on her face has me turning towards the mirror once more, and she tells no lies. I look white as a sheet. Brushing off the eerie feeling, I concentrate on what's in her hands. Half the shop, apparently.

She glances down to where my eyes are bouncing over the different pieces. One looks like it needs more than a master's degree to get in and out of, and she chuckles. "Oh, these are just to see what you're comfortable in and what suits you. You've got a beautiful shape, and I wanted to try these out on you first." She hands me a lacy, black balconette bra and a plunge-line red one with a satin finish. Masie starts jabbering on about her studies and working a job at the same time, something I can relate to, which puts me at ease once more, and she starts getting me in and out of what feels like one hundred pieces of underwear.

Half an hour later, I emerge from the changing room with three new sets and a bodysuit, which will look pretty under a dress. Not all of this is for Paul. I love wearing sexy underwear; it makes me feel sexy and powerful. So, without asking how much they are, I follow Masie to the till and pay for my goods. She even throws in a free spritz thing. God knows what that's for, but I'll find out later when I get home.

I take my time window shopping around the centre, enjoying some me time, and I swing into a store that has a dress in the window I like the look of. As I'm trying to find the rack with it, I feel a hand on my back. My entire body freezes in fear.

"Sorry!" I hear a woman say as she moves out from behind me. "I nearly went straight into you." She heads off in a different direction, and I walk out of the store. I'm not entirely sure why my body is on high alert today, making me jump at little things, but clearly, it's had enough of being out and wants to go home. So homeward bound we go.

When I finally get home, I lock the door behind me and head straight for a hot bath. I had planned to feel sexy and excited for when Paul got back, but instead, I felt frayed and on edge for no reason that I could explain.

The moment I sink into the scalding water, my tense muscles begin to unwind. The heat seeps into my bones, and before I know it, my eyelids grow heavy.

I don't realise I've drifted off until the sound of the front door closing startles me awake. A shiver runs through me as I sit up, suddenly aware that the water around me has turned ice cold.

Chapter Twenty-Three

SOPHIE

Stepping out of the bath and hurriedly wrapping myself in my robe, I hear Paul whistling to himself. The sound of cupboards opening and closing tells me he must have nipped over to the shop. He takes such good care of me.

My pamper time has been cut short…or rather, I cut it short by falling asleep, leaving myself less time to get ready. Instead of indulging in my usual routine, I quickly moisturise, slip into the black lace set I bought today, and tie my robe back around me before heading into the living space.

Paul spins around at the sound of my bare feet padding across the floor.

"Aren't you a sight for sore eyes?"

Just like that, the uneasy feelings from earlier melt away. I never wanted to rely on someone like this again, but here we are. Mr. Charming has officially become my emotional support human.

"Hey, you. Sorry, I didn't realise how late it was. I fell asleep in the bath." The words come out softer than I'd intended, laced with a quiet need for reassurance. Paul steps towards me and wraps his warm arms around my body, pulling me to him and kissing the top of my head.

"You must have needed it, love. You staying wrapped like a present whilst I cook us dinner?" The humour in his voice has me bouncing on the balls of my feet. He kisses me once more and walks over to the fridge. I dutifully follow, wanting to see and taste what we're having.

After we've devoured a beautiful tomato pasta with fresh bread, we half-lay and half-sit on the sofa. Paul's scrolling through emails on his phone, and I'm watching reels of ducklings on mine. In my periphery, I notice Paul glance over at me, back to his phone, and then his head snaps back over to me. I lower my phone, not really sure what's caught his attention, until I see the hunger swirling around his eyes. He leans forward and places his phone on the table in front of him, turning to face me and giving me all of his attention.

I lean up on my elbow, not realising how close to horizontal I actually am, and I look down to see exactly what has caught Paul's eye. The tie to my robe has loosened somewhat, and I am now showing off what I had completely forgotten about. Quite a preview of the new underwear I bought this afternoon.

"When I said you looked like a present," Paul licks his lips, leaning forward to pull my tie free and expose my front to him, "I wasn't expecting this!" His gaze is raking over my body, which is heating up and throbbing in all the right places.

I stand up and move in front of him, allowing my robe to fall off completely. If I could have ever imagined what it'd be like to be worshipped, this is it. Paul's gaze sweeps over me, dark and deliberate, as if he's memorising every inch of lace and skin. His fingers hover near my waist, hesitant, reverent.

"Jesus, Sophie," he breathes, his voice thick with something between awe and hunger.

Warmth spreads through me, pooling deep in my belly. I've never felt so powerful…so utterly seen. His hands finally make contact, gliding over my hips, tracing the delicate fabric, his fingertips barely skimming the lace.

"You did this for me?" he questions quietly.

I shiver. "Maybe."

His lips curve into a knowing smirk as his hands tighten and slide lower, his grip turning possessive. "Then let me show you how much I appreciate it." Paul's fingers slip beneath the lace, teasing and exploring, his touch sending a delicious shiver down my spine. He watches me, drinking in every reaction, every tremor of anticipation.

"You're incredible," he murmurs as he stands, brushing his lips against my collarbone, his breath hot against my skin.

I arch into him, desperate for more, for the heat of his body to chase away the chill creeping over me. My trembling hands find his shoulders, and he groans as I press my body closer to his.

The air between us thickens, charged with the weight of everything unspoken. His hands slide up my back, undoing me in every way that matters.

Then, with a low chuckle, he whispers, "I think we need to get you properly warmed up."

Paul's hands move with purpose now, sliding over my skin like he's relearning every inch of me. His lips trail down my neck, his evening stubble grazing against my sensitive skin, causing a slight shiver throughout my body.

I tilt my head back, giving him more, needing more. My breath catches when his hands slip lower, tracing the curve of my waist, his thumbs brushing the delicate lace at my hips.

"You're feeling rather cold, Soph," he murmurs against my skin, his voice a mix of concern and desire.

I can barely form words, but I manage a breathless "Then warm me up."

His low chuckle vibrates against me, and in one swift motion, he lifts me into his arms. I gasp, wrapping my arms around his neck as he carries me effortlessly toward the bed.

The moment I hit the mattress, he's over me, his body pressing against me, his heat sinking into every chilled part of me. His hands, his mouth, his body... he's everywhere, and it's not just warmth he's giving me. It's worship, devotion, and a kind of fire that starts deep in my core and spreads outward.

I tangle my fingers in his hair, pulling him closer. "Paul…"

He groans against my skin. "Sophie, you have no idea what you do to me."

And then, he shows me.

Twice.

Chapter Twenty-Four

PAUL

As the lovely autumn is rolling to quite a firm end, as in no more nice warm days, it's typical British weather of wet, cold, and grey now. I'm wrestling with my umbrella, laptop bag, and coffee on my way into the office. Christmas is just around the corner, and I'm thinking about what to get Sophie for a present. I've already bought her jewellery, so I don't want to do that again. A spa voucher, perhaps? A little too generic, considering how quickly we've become a couple.

Musing over that thought, I can't remember the last night I spent by myself. Not that I'm complaining. I love her company and spending our evenings together. But before Sophie, I used to have one or two nights just for me. I don't need that now. Is this a growing moment? My parents would be proud.

They've always wanted me to settle down, and since Gavin announced his feelings for Jess, I've heard nothing other than getting a girl, settling down, having babies, etc. Even Gavin's mum asked about my future; Gavin, of course, spilt the beans that I had been seeing one person. That must have been a great conversation for them. I've always been single, not that I don't like women; it's been more about not really wanting a relationship before.

Now that I've found Soph? I honestly can't see my time without her. Does she want kids? She's still cagey about her past. Does she want to get married? These are things I can only assume people normally talk about in relationships.

If I had my way right now, I'd wife her up and never let her go. But we're still treading water, so back to my predicament. What do I get her?

I sit through countless meetings, and still, the question is on my mind at lunch. I pop my head into Gavin's office, and he isn't there. Bloody typical. I try Jess; she is there, and I may say a little jumpy when I walk in.

"Hey, you!" She's a little too chirpy. I mean, she is normally chirpy, but there's an edge to it today.

"What you doing?" I cross my arms and lean against her desk; she looks like she's been caught with her hand in the cookie jar, and she knows it. Rolling her eyes and huffing at me, she finally relents. That didn't take long at all!

"I'm organising a present for Gavin, and it's a surprise before you ask. Do we have a meeting?" She glances over to her laptop and back to me.

"No, but I could do with some of your woman's intuition." Leaning back in her chair, Jess folds her hands on her lap and listens intently whilst I jabber away about wanting to get Sophie something special. I don't miss her glowing smile as I talk.

After a good twenty minutes of hashing things out, I have a plan. Well, four ideas. In no particular order… A pair of earrings to go with the necklace I bought in Paris…not bad, but that might be an opener. A sex voucher book…I mean, I love the idea, but I'd rather make my own vouchers rather than one of those books. An experience and something we can do together…nothing immediately springs to mind, which says to me that I need to get to know her a little more than how her body sings for me. Loudly, I might add. And last but not least, a grand gesture…what that gesture could be, Jess was pretty useless with. I have no idea, so I'm just as useless. But there are my four ideas, and I don't have long at all to sort it out.

So, I push that to the back of my mind for now. It'll come to me at some point. I hope. I dig my phone out of my pocket whilst sitting back down at my desk. There is one way I can find out.

Me: What do you want for Christmas?

Sophie: What? Lol. Are we doing presents then?

Me: Don't you want a present?

Sophie: Always!! What do you want?

Me: I have no idea. You.

Sophie: Haha. You already have me.

Me: You avoided my questions.

Sophie: Yep!

Me: Tell me...

I waited ten minutes for a response before I gave up. She is a stubborn little minx. Either that or she is like me and has no idea what to say because I tend to buy what I want or need. I'm actually quite hard to buy for, which may explain some of the previous years' Secret Santa presents. There are only so many ties, pens, and golf related paraphernalia you can have as gifts.

Shit. What do I want? I wrack my brain whilst making a cup of coffee. Who said men can't multitask, eh? Then it hits me. I was honest in my text. There's only one thing I do want.

Sophie.

Shit.

Chapter Twenty-Five

SOPHIE

After Paul's messages, I start to look at the lists I'd already started building on my favourite online shops. He doesn't want for anything—that I do know—but after spending so much time with him and in his apartment, I have silly things in my lists: throw cushions that are so colourful they could turn you blind, whimsical whiskey glasses, a nice bottle of whiskey.

I also don't want to get him anything too serious that might scare him off because, if I'm honest, these feelings have been catching hotter than a wildfire, and although that is worrying given my history, everything in me is screaming that this is right. That we're right together. Throwing caution into the wind, I move the printed canvas into my basket. We may only have the odd selfie together, but the picture I've chosen is quite nice, and I'm hoping he'll like it.

Whilst my brain is on the subject of Christmas, I fire off a message to my sister and dad. I'd love to see them over the holidays this year. I normally say I'm working, and during previous holidays, I suppose I have been. But I have a much better work/life balance now, and I want to go home for a few days. It's been way too long since I properly spent time with them. I make a note in my diary to get some nice flowers for Mum's grave, too. I haven't spoken with her for a long time, let alone visited her grave. It's like ignoring it happened, contacting my family as little as possible and not really going home has been my way of pretending mum isn't dead.

That thought prompts me to add a reminder to contact a therapist to schedule something for after Christmas. I can't keep avoiding my grief, pain, or Cardiff, but if I'm going to break down, I'm going to make sure I'm with a professional when I do.

The office is quiet today, and I'm feeling a little exposed after those thoughts. Instead of staying, I pack my stuff and make my way home for the afternoon. Not just because of the thoughts. The satin red bra I bought? As comfortable as a brick. It was fine walking around in it, but who in their right mind decided that a bra needed bones all the way around? I'm nearly a hundred per cent sure I have bruises, and I cannot wait to get home and whip it off. Stupid, pretty underwear that isn't practical to wear on a daily basis.

Naturally, I stop by the green mermaid coffee haven on my way home for something sweet and a latte. It'd be rude not to, after all, especially with the pain it's going to cause putting this bra back in the drawer, not to be worn again after it cost a small fortune. As I'm walking back out with my to-go cup in hand, still on my internal rant cursing underwear manufacturers, I smell something sickeningly familiar. It smells like bergamot and something woody; I never found out what type of wood smell. But it smells like *him*. It takes my brain a moment to connect back with my body, but I am frozen in place. I force myself to move; it's just a coincidence. Lots of men have this aftershave. It doesn't stop my eyes from darting around, scanning the area for a glimpse of what should be impossible.

Have I become too comfortable? Too distracted with Paul? I have been vigilant for years, ensuring I'm not in crowds for long, just in case I'm in the background of a photo. You can change your hair colour, but other than shoving contacts in—which is something I didn't want to do—there is no way I can change my eyes, and there's no way I would have considered reconstruction to change my physical appearance. He knows my appearance and eyes well after being in my face for years. Shouting and threatening me. I suppose, technically, he did change the colour of my face on a couple of occasions. But that's something I don't want to think about right now.

As my gaze lands on a couple holding hands, sitting outside near the door, I breathe in through my nose, and I smell it. I smile politely and lean in towards them.

"Excuse me, I couldn't help but notice the aftershave you're wearing."

The man with dark hair turns to me and smiles.

"Aww thank you! Gerrard here bought it for my birthday." Pointing to his partner. "It's Savuage by Dior."

"Oh, thank you. I'll make a mental note of that. Have a great afternoon!" Smiling brightly, the bile threatens to come up my oesophagus.

It wasn't him. It wasn't him. It wasn't him.

You're safe. For now.

Fuck my life. I'm going to go home, lock that bloody door, and get through some drawings before Paul gets home. Huh. Home. Interesting. Well, we're either at my place or his, but I may suggest we stay at his tonight just to make me feel a little safer. I'm not sure what excuse I'll give, but it'll be a nice change anyway. We've been at mine for a week, and besides, one of my favourite pairs of joggers is at his.

Are they mine? No. Do I wear them anyway because I like wearing Paul's clothes? Absolutely yes.

> Me: I'm missing my joggers. You ok if I head to yours to work this afternoon and we sleep there tonight?

> Paul: You mean my joggers, which you look bloody hot in. But absolutely fine, love. Tied up in meetings until 4 then will make my way to you.

> Me: See you later x

Awesome! I make my way back to my flat to pack a couple of bits and head over to Paul's. I'll get my work done there, and I somehow feel a little safer in his ivory tower.

Chapter Twenty-Six

PAUL

I walk through my front door to the smell of toast. I swear to God, if this woman is going to tell me beans on toast is an evening meal, I'm going to have to have words. Stepping my way through into the kitchen, I hear Soph singing away, and low and behold, there are plates with toast. I laugh when I see the chef's swoosh, which I can only assume is the tomato sauce from the beans with three beans placed on it. I mean, A for effort.

I clear my throat, making her turn around with a megawatt grin as she sees the amused expression on my face.

"I'm elevating dinner!" she says in a sweet voice as she pours the rest of the beans in a neat pile onto the plate and adds a slice of prosciutto ham on top. This is it; I'm actually having beans on toast for my dinner. I haven't had this since I was a child, but my mum didn't raise an arsehole, and I sit my ass down and eat.

"I really don't want to admit this, but that was actually quite enjoyable and filling," I say, wiping my plate clean with the last piece of my toast.

"I'm also not going to say I told you so. But I did." Soph leans back in her chair as I clear the plates away. One good thing about this dinner is that only one pan was used to make it, which means there is barely anything to tidy away.

"What made you want to come here today?" I'm genuinely intrigued. I'm not complaining about being at home, but she always seemed comfortable at hers.

"I told you, I wanted my favourite joggers," she says, pulling at the waistband of my joggers, that are at least 2 sizes too big for her. There's an edge to her voice; something I can't quite put my finger on.

"You sure? You sound different, love." I potter around her, not wanting to make her feel uncomfortable, but I'd like to think I'm easy to talk to, and the fact my place seems to be a space of solace for her. Sophie starts fidgeting, and I know my gut instincts are right. Something has riled her today.

"It's going to sound crazy…" she starts, and I put down the last of the dishes and walk over to her to hold her hand. It's mainly to help the fidgeting but to also let her know I'm here. "…but there was a smell that triggered a bad memory, and I wanted to be surrounded by you." Sophie's voice is barely a whisper by the end of her sentence. I don't push for more. Instead, I wrap her in my arms.

"Then I'll surround you with me. I'm here, Soph. We may not have said it aloud, but I think we both know that this isn't a fling. I'm not going anywhere." Sophie's body sags against mine, and I lift her chin and place a soft kiss on her lips. We pad over to the sofa, and I let her choose something to watch. I'm lucky enough to not have many bad memories, but I'm feeling like a peacock at the moment, knowing that I'm her safe space, her person. I watch her out of the corner of my eye as she touches the necklace I bought her in Paris. She hasn't taken it off once, and my chest swells with the knowledge that she carries a piece of me each day.

***

SCREAMING. THAT'S WHAT I HEAR AS I'M DRAGGED from a deep sleep. I jump into an upright position, letting my eyes adjust to the darkness surrounding me. I look over at Sophie, who is sweating, twisted up in the sheets, and panting hard.

Did she scream?

My question is answered again when a blood-curdling scream comes out of her mouth. Her face is twisted in pain, and I feel my heart constrict watching her. I know you're not supposed to wake someone from a nightmare, but I can't leave her trapped in her head. Therefore, I do what I do most nights when she's having a nightmare; I pull her into me and stroke her hair, shushing her and telling her she's safe and with me.

Tonight, though, it's not working. She starts thrashing against me, and I realise that restricting her may not have been the best move. I release her from my arms and talk a little louder, hoping to reach the part of her brain that knows this is only a nightmare. I glance at my phone on the bedside table, 2:22am. I'm sure it was around this time she had one before. Sophie is still struggling in her dream, so I quickly google what to do.

Reassure—done. Offer comfort—didn't work. Don't forcefully wake—it's getting harder by the second.

She's screaming and mumbling, "No, not again. Please stop."

Honestly, it's breaking my heart. Apparently, I'm meant to guide her back to a peaceful sleep. I place my hand over her heart, making sure I don't put too much pressure on her so she doesn't feel restrained, and I stroke her hair with my other hand.

"Sophie, it's Paul. You're okay. You're safe." I repeat these words for five painful minutes before I feel her heartbeat slow down. Once I feel her relax a little, I go into the bathroom and run a flannel under the cold tap. By the time I'm back in bed, she's murmuring so quietly I can't hear the words.

Slowly and gently, I wipe away the sweat and tears from her face, cooling her down a little. When she's starting to look less clammy, I place the flannel on her bedside table and pull her into me, talking in a soft voice, telling her that she's safe. She's with me. When I feel her hand squeeze my arm, I raise my head to see her blinking back at me.

"Paul…" Her voice sounds broken, partly from the screaming and partly from that fact it's gone 2:30am.

"Sophie, you're safe. I've got you." I hold her tighter now that she's awake. Sophie turns to bury her face in my chest, and her body is wracked with sobs. I hold her close to me, stroking her hair, and when the sobs subside, Sophie lifts her head a little.

"I think I need to tell you about Cardiff," she says, her voice so quiet you wouldn't hear it if there was any background noise.

Part of me is glad she's going to tell me, and the other part is terrified about what I'm about to find out.

Chapter Twenty-Seven

SOPHIE

Howard made us a picnic. So romantic! We are by the sea wall, stars twinkling above us, and there is barely a soul in sight. It's like he knew the perfect, private spot for us. And what girl doesn't love wine, cheese, meat, and bread?

Sipping my wine, I lean back against the wall and stare out at the sea. Well, channel, really, but it opens out into the sea. His hand grazes mine, snapping my attention from the water to his eyes. Those muddy brown eyes look almost black in this light. I shiver as I think about how primal he looks, bordering on danger-ous. But I know Howard is sweet. We've been on a few dates, and he hasn't pressured me about sex. He's only given me gentle-manly kisses. Tonight, though, I want that to change.

"Keep looking at me like that, Soph, and I'm going to end up devouring you." I bite my lip at the threat and promise and don't look away, challenging him to make good on his words. He leans in, takes my wine from me, and places it down behind him. When those dark orbs are back on me, I feel my heart skipping a beat. I lean forward, desperate to feel him against me.

"Soph…" His voice sounds desperate, but I don't want to hear the rest. I push myself further, pressing my lips to his, and as if some restraint has snapped, he pushes me onto my back and kisses me like he has never done before. This feels rough and needy, and I feel downright sexy. I rock my hips into his, wanting to feel him, and, my god, do I feel him. One hand whips down to my hip, holding it in place with a bruising grip. I whimper into his mouth, which makes his hand tighten. Did he mistake it for me liking it? I mean, it's not too painful, but it does hurt.

He comes up for air, leaving my lips feeling bruised and swollen, both of us panting. The hand on my hip is now brushing up and down my side. "I'm going to take you back to mine, Soph, and you're going to be such a good girl for me."

The anticipation I feel is vibrating through my body, making the throbbing between my legs so much worse. I need some relief. I nod in agreement, and we pack our picnic and head back to his car.

I WAKE UP FEELING GROGGY, HUNGOVER AND disorientated. I only had a couple of glasses of wine, but I can't remember what happened after leaving the sea wall. Did I miss having sex for the first time? As if on cue, my body reels off everything that hurts. Oh my God, I'm in so much pain. My boobs feel like they've been used as a punching bag. My ribs, why do they hurt? My head is killing me, my pussy feels so bruised, and my ass… Oh fuck, why does it hurt?

I try to sit up, but I can't. I hear a dark chuckle near me, somewhere in the darkness of this room. It smells damp and *mouldy. Is this where Howard lives? He could do with some air freshener.*

"About time you woke up. I was bored of fucking a warm corpse." Bile comes up so quickly I can't stop the vomit spewing from my mouth. Fuck, even my stomach feels bruised. His voice sounds full of venom. I see movement and try to shuffle back, but I realise now that I'm tied down. My brain is desperately trying to fill in the gaps, but it doesn't have to try hard for too long.

I'm pushed back, and his cock is being forced into me. The tearing feeling brings fresh tears to my eyes. "Stop, please."

He just laughs, punches me in the ribs, and turns me over to tear my ass more. I don't know when I stop pleading with him, but I just lie there, unable to escape the pain. I'm punched and taken, beaten and choked. What did I do wrong? We were having a nice time, weren't we?

When he finally finishes, he unties my bonds and throws me to the floor, kicking me until I'm screaming. The pain radiating through my body is too much.

At the highest point, I feel someone soothing me and talking to me. The pain slowly subsides. I hear him…Paul. This is a nightmare. I'm with Paul. I'm safe. I can walk out of this room. I hear Paul repeating that I'm safe. The darkness subsides and fades into the light. I feel his body wrapped around mine as I slowly float back into consciousness. I need to tell him. He needs to know this part of me. I'm starting to fall for him, and I'd rather he leave me now than later down the line. Paul…

PAUL HAS MADE US BOTH A CUPPA, AND WE'RE SAT cuddled in bed. I'm surrounded by him and his scent, and I feel safe. I take in a shaky, deep breath, ready to tell him. We're leaning against his headboard, and he puts his arm around me and takes my spare hand in his. Does he realise how reassuring he is?

I take a sip of my drink and gather my courage with my breath. "I started university in Cardiff not long after my mum died. I tried to escape the guilt of leaving my dad and sister at home to deal with their own feelings whilst I ignored mine. Losing her broke my heart. I felt abandoned and alone. I'd already been accepted for my architect degree and didn't want to postpone. I thought keeping myself busy would help, you know?"

Paul squeezes my hand and stays silent, letting me continue. "After a few months of burying myself in coursework and lectures, I started to go to socials, wanting to build a network of friends so I didn't feel alone. That's when I met *him*. He was sweet. A gentleman. I felt special…seen…like I was the centre of his universe. He'd bring me roses. Once, I pricked myself on one of the thorns, and he laughed a little whilst wiping my blood. I thought he laughed because I was clumsy. I was wrong." My chest shudders with my next breath, I've never told anyone about Howard. Some of it was out of fear, some of it was avoidance.

"He started to take me on dates. All of them were sweet and romantic. He never pressured me into anything. He kissed me like a gentleman and said goodnight. Until one night by the sea wall. We were having a picnic under the stars, and I wanted more. We kissed, like properly kissed, and he took me back to his. I don't remember most of it…only waking up in pain and restrained." I feel Paul go rigid beside me; his grip on my hand is still light, but his body is hard and stiff.

"I spent years thinking this was my fault. I still do. It wouldn't have happened if I hadn't wanted to have sex. But when I woke up, my body was beaten, and I found out he'd had sex with me when I was unconscious. When I finally came around, he did it again and again. Then beat me more.

"I must have passed out because when I woke up, he was different. He was the most charming man I'd met. He'd bought me flowers, apologised for being rough, and said he cared for me. We spent the next week at his house; he wouldn't let me leave with my bruises. He said people would ask questions, and I wouldn't want to let anyone know how clumsy I'd been. He was a perfect gentleman for a few days. I thought it was all in my head and that I'd had a bad dream. Then it happened again. The room we stayed in when he hurt me was damp, dark, and smelt like mould. It wasn't his bedroom; that was light and airy. Thinking back, Howard was like Jekyll and Hyde. One side was romantic, light, and fun, and the other was dark, dangerous, and full of pain."

I take a moment, my drink easing my sore throat. Paul stays quiet, letting go of me only to take a sip of his drink. I dare not look at his face. I don't want to know he's checked out of this relationship yet. I just want to finish telling him about Cardiff, then I'll get dressed and go home. No one wants to be with someone who's broken. That's one piece of shitty advice Howard gave me. One that never left.

"For years, we went through this cycle. In public, we were the perfect couple. Behind closed doors, I went through weeks of being hurt. My ribs had been cracked numerous times, and my body endured multiple assaults from him. If I had a nightmare, he'd hit me, telling me I was a stupid bitch for waking him up. After my third year, I was allowed to celebrate with my friends. A very small circle of people I'd gotten to know through my classes. I wasn't allowed many friends. No one could know about what happened between us in private. He used to say that was our business. I had a couple of glasses of wine when we were celebrating our results after our fourth year, and when he came to meet me, I knew I had been bad. I wasn't allowed to drink because, apparently, it made me talkative. Not that I would have told anyone what he did to me. He always said it was my fault." Paul's hand momentarily squeezes a little too hard, and I flinch.

"I'm sorry, love. I didn't mean to hurt you. Please, continue." Paul's hand relaxes, but I swear I feel the anger rolling off of him.

"My last year of uni, I barely attended classes. My professors were very kind and let me work from home. Well, not my home. His. Where he'd watch me constantly. He did his work from there, too, to keep an eye on me so I didn't do anything stupid. When I passed my degree with honours, I was honestly surprised. Pleased but surprised. Howard told me which architectural firms I was allowed to apply to, but I sneakily applied to the one where I work now. I wanted to escape. I didn't want to be near him. The whole time I was at university, I couldn't escape him. But now I could. The day before I left, I packed up my stuff and sent it to my flat. I'd rented that without him finding out. I changed my name—well, my last name anyway—and hoped he wouldn't find out. On my last night, he went out drinking. He'd crushed something in my drink before he left, but I poured it away. When he forgot to lock the door, I knew that was my chance to escape. When I could, I ran. I didn't risk getting a taxi from his place. I went into the centre of town and took the train from there to London. As soon as I picked up my keys, I went to the shop and bought dye for my hair, thinking that if my name wasn't enough, surely changing my appearance would help. I've been hiding ever since."

"Soph…" Paul's voice is soft, his tone caring.

"A few weeks ago, there were rose petals all the way from Starbucks to my flat. A bare rose stem was left on my doorstep. I've been feeling jumpy, and when I smelt his aftershave yesterday, I panicked. He can't have found me, but I wanted to feel safe."

Letting out a shuddery breath, I sink into Paul's side, feeling like this is the last time I will tell this story and the last night we will spend together.

Chapter Twenty-Eight

PAUL

If anyone had told me that one day I would feel a rage that shook my entire existence, a rage that made me want to murder someone in cold blood and enjoy it, I would have been shocked and probably laughed at them before I shook it off.

But at nearly four in the morning, I am vibrating with such rage. I knew something had happened in Cardiff, but never, NEVER, would I have imagined something so dark…so evil had threatened this wonderful woman.

I am still reeling from Sophie's story. Her history. The reason she dyes her hair. The reason she's been jumpy and doesn't have a lot at her house. It probably makes it easier to pack up and run again. As I process the details, Sophie puts her cup on her bedside table and gets up. It isn't until she's getting dressed that I fully realise what's happening.

"What are you doing?" I focus on her as she's

putting stuff in a bag. Is she packing? It's stupid o'clock in the morning, and she's just revealed a fuck tonne of trauma. I stand up and walk over to her, gently tilting her chin to get her to look at me. Her eyes are brimming with tears, and her body looks small in my joggers and t-shirt. "Soph, what are you doing?" I say a little gentler this time.

She wipes away a tear that's fallen down her cheek, straightens her back, and fixes me with a blank stare. It's like she's shut away the vulnerable part of herself that was here just a moment ago.

"I'm going to go home. No one wants something that's broken." More tears fall from her glistening eyes as she talks. She sounds robotic. Numb.

"You ain't going anywhere, love." I see a flash of fear in her face and curse myself. That's what he did. Kept her locked away. "As in, you aren't leaving here tonight. If you want space tomorrow, that's fine. But tonight, you're staying here. And for that bullshit comment of 'no one wants anything that's broken', that's bullshit, Soph. I'm here. I'm yours. Thank you for telling me. I should have said that first, but it's up to me whether I want you. And I. Want. You. All of you."

More tears fall down her beautiful face, and I swipe them away with my thumbs whilst cradling her face in my hands. As if I'd let her go. She's mine. Not in a dickhead way that he thought she was his, but she is mine. If she thinks revealing her past would make me want her less, then she will learn in time. Her time.

"But…I'm broken." Her voice breaks as the tears free fall.

"We're all broken in some way, love. But it's how we put ourselves back together that makes us who we are, and when you find someone who makes you feel whole again, you don't let them go. You make me feel whole, Sophie. I'm not letting you go."

She lunges at me, holding me tightly as if I'll fade away if she doesn't. When my ribs start to complain, I push her away a little, grab her hand, and take her back to bed, where I hold her, surrounding her in my strength and feelings. Hopefully, it will make her feel safe enough to stay.

I COME ROUND FEELING EXHAUSTED, AND WHEN I REACH over to Sophie's side of the bed, I find it empty and cold. I turn to check the time on my phone, 11am. Shit! I fire a text off to Gavin saying I'll work from home and had a rough night, knowing full well he'll be fine, and then I jump out of bed in search of Sophie.

I don't have to go too far before I find her on the sofa with her laptop open. The smell of coffee penetrates my nostrils as I run my fingers through my hair. The worry flowing through me starts to subside as I watch her for a moment. I kiss the top of her head as I pass her to move into the kitchen. I need caffeine in my system as I sort through the mixture of emotions in my head. How on earth she copes with the nightmares and then a full day of work with very little sleep is beyond me.

"Hi," she says softly, not looking up from her laptop.

"Morning," I offer as I plonk myself next to her.

She shyly glances my way, opens and closes her mouth, and slowly closes her laptop. "Paul, I'm sorry about last night. I'm a lot, and I don't want you to feel that you have to stay with me. Especially if it's out of pity." Her speech sounds rehearsed like she's been thinking about it since she woke up.

"Soph, we're in this together now. I appreciate that you trust me enough to have told me about your past. It must have been an incredibly scary and traumatic time, but please trust me when I tell you that I am not with you out of pity." I sip my coffee, scalding my tongue slightly. "I'm with you for your body."

She laughs loudly, and I feel myself lighten with the sound. Last night was heavy, and I didn't want to belittle it in any way, but I did want to make her more relaxed. Mission accomplished.

"For fucks sake, Paul." She bats my arm. "I was being serious."

"So was I." I shrug and head back to the bedroom to chuck on some clothes before setting up my laptop for the day. When I get back to the living room, Sophie is engrossed in something on her screen resembling a building, and I sit on the other side of the sofa and open up my emails. My phone pings with a text from Gavin:

Gavin: No worries, mate. Hope you're alright. Catch you later.

Legend, that man. Although he's my best friend,

he's also the best boss. I fire through my emails in no time and get stuck on the budgets for the next fiscal year. By the time I looked up from my laptop, it was gone four, and Soph had nodded off, her laptop still open. I get up to stretch my legs and close her laptop, leaving her to sleep for another hour or so before I order dinner. Neither of us has eaten today, and I'm way too exhausted to cook.

Chapter Twenty-Nine

SOPHIE

For two days we worked from Paul's apartment. Two days of feeling safe, comforted, and like a huge weight had been lifted from my shoulders. As I walk into the office, Richard gives me a smile and brings me a coffee.

"How are you feeling, Sophie?" he asks, perching on my desk.

"Much better, thanks. I just needed a couple of days couped up to finish this project." Which isn't a complete lie, but he doesn't need to know the details. We chat nonsense for a few minutes before his phone rings and pulls him away from my desk.

I spend the morning tidying my desk, filing completed projects, and organising my to-do tray when lunch comes around. The team is heading to the pub, and I join them. Since we've all found a new groove and the misogynistic atmosphere has left us, I feel like I'm a part of the team and welcome. I actually enjoy spending time with them now. Even Richard, who, after telling me about his shitty dad, is a pretty nice guy.

I order a mouthwatering burger for lunch and devour it like an animal; Paul and I have been eating a lot at his, but I'm hungry. Lunchtime is full of laughter, especially when I let slip that I called Josh's drawings Mickey Mouse drawings in my head. I like this, the comradery, the gentle ribbing of each other without it being sexist or derogatory. On our way back to the office, Richard slings his arm around me, and we chat about a girl he's got his eye on. He wants advice on how to be a better guy and how to properly date her. It's sweet, and to think, the man who used to be the reason I hated coming into the office is now friendly and asking advice about women. It's wonderful when people want to evolve. So, I give him some ideas, like starting off small with a coffee and then going to dinner on another date. Pretty much like Paul and I did. Build a foundation first rather than get her drunk, and then wham bam, thank you, ma'am!

Sitting back down at my desk, our receptionist brings over a bunch of flowers. My instinct is to freeze, but I thank her, take the flowers, and read the card.

Soph,
Just because I miss you.
Paul x

I take a look at the flowers again; there's not one

rose in sight. Instead, I have yellow sunflowers, pink carnations, white baby's breath, and yellowy-orange alstroemeria. Bright, beautiful, and colourful. I feel my eyes sting with emotion as the thoughtfulness of the flowers hits me. Damn, he's wonderful.

> Me: The flowers are beautiful. Thank you so much x

> Paul: Not as beautiful as you x

Smooth, Paul, damn smooth. I put my phone down, pop the flowers into a temporary vase—it's a pint glass, but still—and crack on with my afternoon. Today feels like a great day. Hopefully, one of many to come.

I HAVE A SPRING IN MY STEP AS I GET CLOSER TO HOME. Paul and I decided to stay apart tonight as much as it actually pains me. But he's got meetings followed by his work Christmas party, and then an early morning, and I'm heading home to spend some time with my dad and sister tomorrow. It's crazy how quickly Christmas time has come, but Paul and I are doing our own little Christmas when I get back from my family visit.

As I near my local coffee haven, I smell that berg-amot scent that brings bile to my throat. Last time, I panicked, and it turned out to be another man. So, instead of freezing, I walk ahead and into Starbucks to get myself a latte to celebrate a wonderful day. As the barista calls my name, I grab my latte with one hand

and keep my beautiful flowers in the other. Using my hip to open the door, I accidentally brush someone walking by, and it feels like every single hair on my body is standing on end.

"Love the new hair, Soph." *His* voice sounds light and rich, but I know better. I know this man doesn't do light and relaxed. It only leads to dark things.

"Changing your name made it a little harder to find you, but I did. I hope you liked the roses I left you." I *knew* those internal warning signs were for a reason. The rose that was delivered to work and the petals leading from Starbucks to my home. Fuck! How long has he been following me?

"Howard." I try to push past him, but he grabs my arm and pulls me to his chest, the smell of that after-shave infiltrating my senses, trying to pull me into the darkness of that awful room. NO! I'm not going back there; I'm not being abused. It took me too long to heal, too long to trust. Too long to love…

"Let's go for a little walk." His voice takes a sinister tone as he practically drags me towards my flat. When we reach my building, and he punches in the code, fear strikes through me as if I've been struck by lightning.

"How long have you been following me?" I feel brave, clutching the flowers Paul sent me with all my might. I fear I may break them.

"Long enough to know you've been a slut." Glaring down at me with those dark mud-brown eyes, he drags me through the door and up to my apartment. I don't need to get my keys from my bag; he already has one cut.

Fuck! Fuck! Fuck!

"Aw, Soph, it looks like you're already packed for our trip."

Fear covers me. Everyone is expecting me to be away for a couple of days. How long will it take them to notice I'm not back? Will my dad and sister think I've just not turned up?

Shit!

Chapter Thirty

Walking out of my client's office, I stretch my neck. I feel tense from sitting in one position for hours, but it was a worthwhile meeting. Did it need to take three hours, though? Absolutely not. The majority of that could have been an email, but here we are. Instead of taking a taxi back to the office, I walk back, allowing the fresh December air to clear my mind. Last night's party was fun, and I'm thankful I didn't drink too much, either. I couldn't have gotten through that meeting if I was hungover, but I'm still tired.

It's nearing on lunchtime and as I consider what to have for lunch, Sophie pops into my mind. She should be getting to her dad's house soon as she would have left a couple of hours ago, I send her a quick message to let her know that one, I'm thinking of her, and two, I miss her.

Me: Let me know when you get to
your dad's, love. Can't wait to see you
in a couple of days. Speak to you
later xx

There's a prickle in my stomach when I check my phone ten minutes later, and I see the message sits on read. She normally responds when she reads a message, or she'll leave it unread to respond to later. She probably got distracted. I know it's been a while since she's seen her dad and sister.

When Soph opened up to me about Cardiff, she told me about the guilt she'd been carrying for years, avoiding her grief and, in turn, avoiding her dad and sister. The fact she's going to see them for a couple of days, spending time with them, and going to visit her mum's grave is a huge step for her. In the new year, I'm going to suggest she see a therapist to help with her guilt, grief, and trauma. Not because I don't think she can cope, but I honestly think it'll help her heal and move past it.

I'm so caught up in my head thinking about Soph that I don't realise I'm back in the office until I'm taking my coat off. How much of my journey was on autopilot? A lot of it, apparently. I shake off my thoughts and get stuck into work. It's going to be a busy day, and I want to get ahead before the Christmas break. Just as I get into a rhythm, Gavin knocks on the door frame and brings me a coffee. Good man.

"How you doing?" I hold my hand out for the coffee, and he sits down.

"Not bad, could do with a week's sleep," he says with a chuckle. I glance at him for a moment. Yes, he looks tired. We all are after last night, but there's a twinkle in his eye that makes me smile.

"Same. Honestly, though, are we getting old? I'm sure it didn't feel like this a couple of years ago." Leaning back in my chair, I sip on my drink as Gavin does the same.

"Well, I'd like to think we're more distinguished more than getting old." We laugh and reminisce about our younger years. It's not often that we get the time for breaks like this, but when we do, we enjoy every moment.

It's gone seven in the evening when I finally get through my door. I'm totally wiped out and thankful I have leftovers in the fridge to heat up for dinner. But first, I need a shower to wash off today. It hasn't been a terrible day; it's just been long and busy. I'm looking forward to an early night.

When I step out of the shower, I reach for my phone. I still haven't heard from Sophie and decide to send her another text.

Me: Hope you're ok love. Let me know you got to your dads safe x

I chuck on Sophie's favourite joggers and heat up dinner. Who doesn't love lasagne re-heated? Once I have my warmed-up pasta, I sit on the sofa. It feels oddly empty without Sophie sitting on the other end. Missing her more than I thought I could miss another human, I flick on the TV and watch a documentary. David Attenborough never fails to make me feel happy; the man is a legend.

It's now gone nine, and I am just about to head to bed when I get a message. Finally, I was starting to worry. Sophie gave me her dad's address and phone number just in case I couldn't reach her, and I'll be honest to say I wanted to call him to check that she was okay. I read her message twice. It's only a few words, but something feels different. Some people say you can't read a tone or whatever over messages, but when you're used to speaking to someone daily, you get a feeling when something is off.

Sophie: Got here safe. Speak soon x

I hit the call button, and her phone goes straight to voicemail. She never turns her phone off or lets it run down, but then I get another message.

Very little signal, talk tomorrow x

I decided to go to sleep and talk to her tomorrow. I'm probably overtired and reading into something that isn't there. As my head hits the pillow, I get a waft of Sophie's scent from her side of the bed, and it settles me into a much-needed deep sleep.

Chapter Thirty-One

SOPHIE

My body aches. I do a quick mental check from my head to my toes. Yep, everything hurts. I'm surprised I don't have a concussion with how hard my head hit the wall tonight, but something up in the universe is on my side because, although my pain levels are at a nine, adrenaline is pumping through me, telling me I can run.

He's gone out. He told me not to wait up for him, not that that makes a difference. He abuses me whether I'm asleep or awake. But that does mean he won't be back for hours. He'd had a couple of drinks tonight. Cheap vodka that smelt like paint stripper on his breath as he tried to tell me how much he loved me. I look over at the roses he bought; it's like he knows he's going to hurt me and has them on standby.

Every beating, every assault, there are roses. I used to love them. I loved the way the petals formed, the way they smelt, their vibrant colours. But now, they only make me feel sick. It's his way of apologising and making it up to me, knowing full well he's going to do it again. Bastard.

When he left me in the mouldy, damp room, I listened intently. He didn't lock the door this time. Maybe because he thought I was drugged. I mean, he did crush something into my drink, but the thing about being in this room is that everything is already damp. So, when I poured the contents of the plastic cup —because I'm not allowed glass—into the wall, I watched it drain down a little, but it didn't look any different than before.

With Howard thinking I was going into a drug-induced sleep, he didn't lock the door. His car left five minutes ago, and there's been nothing since. I quietly get up off the mattress and test the door.

It is unlocked! A part of me thought I'd missed him locking it, but the hope flowing through my body is now spurring me onto my next step. Get upstairs and find something to put on my feet. He is very insistent when we come back to this hell hole that I take my shoes off at the door. He's allowed his on, but I'm not allowed mine. I'm guessing it's because if I did escape, I couldn't get far barefoot or in socks across the stony path or through the woods.

I sneak upstairs and find a pair of my trainers stashed underneath the sofa, but the bastard has taken the laces out. They'll have to do, though, because I'm not wasting time searching for laces. I grab a bag, leaving mine where it is so he doesn't notice it's missing. I do take my laptop and some books out of it, not wanting to weigh myself down too much. I take a quick look around to make sure nothing seems out of place; I want to get a good head start before he comes for me.

When I feel confident there's nothing left to take, I slowly walk to the front door. Fear spikes through me as I try the front door. I pause, my hand hovering over the door handle. Is this a test? Is he waiting on the other side? Another excuse to punish me? I listen, holding my breath, and when I can't hear anything other than my own erratic heartbeat, I try the door handle.

It opens. I feel the fresh air hitting my face. Although the wind isn't strong today, it feels like it could knock me down. It's been days since I've been allowed outside. I try not to let fear grip and overtake me. I have a plan, and I need to stick to it. Otherwise, he'll find me and drag me back.

He doesn't often lock the front door. There are no neighbours, and no one would come out this way to break into an old, abandoned-looking house.

I step outside and shut the door, energy from fear, hope and a little excitement coursing through my body. I can finally be free!

I tread lightly around the house to the driveway, not wanting to leave any footprints that aren't his leaving the house. When I hit the stone drive, I hold onto the straps of the bag and run.

The wind whips through my hair, and the cuts on my face sting as the tears flow down my face. I'm terrified he'll come back early. I'm terrified he'll figure out my plan and be waiting for me at the station. But I run, regardless. This is my only chance. If I get caught, he'll kill me. He's threatened it before. To kill me, that is, but the bastard never let me die on the days I begged. He enjoyed torturing me too much.

Last week, he brought someone back to the house. I was downstairs in the damp room. He'd been sure to duct tape my mouth before he went on the hunt. Apparently, he doesn't find me sexy anymore. My body isn't what he wants. It doesn't stop him from taking me, though. Time and time again. Last time, I felt my skin tear, and I bled for quite a while after that one. He told me I was disgusting and my body should respond to him with the "pleasure" he gave me.

I heard someone moaning and then screaming his name. I

heard her telling him that was the best head she'd ever had. So, he did remember how to warm someone up. Just not me. I wanted to feel angry, but I felt sad that another girl had fallen for his charm. I hoped she'd be able to leave. When I heard a car pull up an hour later and her leave, I felt relief. For her, anyway. It was soon replaced with fear when his heavy boots came thudding to the door at the top of the stairs.

I brush away the memories as I near the station. I look like shit, but I managed to buy my tickets. My travel costs a fortune, but the one thing about being locked up is that I never spent any money. I walk to the platform; the night train leaves in five minutes. Five minutes of me feeling nauseous, constantly searching the entrance of the station. When I hear the chugging of the train, I feel like I could faint. It's not until I head to the sleeper cabin and the train pulls away from the station that I actually relax. I'm free. I have a couple of hours before I change at the next station, so I take advantage of the bathroom and wash. I can't remember the last time I washed myself with more than a flannel and bucket.

The spare clothes I'd shoved in my bag are clean at least, so when I emerge from the shower room, I feel like a new woman. And when I get to my new place, I will be. Sophie Taylor won't exist any longer. Sophie Martin will take her place and be a different person. When my next station comes up, I don't go to the platform that will take me to Edinburgh. Instead, I buy a ticket to London and never look back.

Yesterday, I got my results. After years of hard work, regardless of the hell I've been in, I passed with honours. Today, I'm running, hopefully, towards a future that doesn't include a dark, mouldy room.

Chapter Thirty-Two

PAUL

It's been two days since I saw Sophie. The messages yesterday left me with an uneasy feeling, and even though I drifted into a deep sleep, it was troubled. My exhaustion took over, and my dreams were full of intrusive thoughts. What if something has happened? What if? What if? What if? What if he found her?

My blood turns to ice at the thought of her ex locating her. The logical part of my brain is trying to reason that he wouldn't bother after all this time. The other part of my brain is wondering what a man would do after having that much control over someone. How would he have felt after finding her gone? Would he spend all these years searching for her? If he has found her, I don't want to imagine what he will do to her. Sophie spent years fearing for her life when she was with him.

I get up from my desk and head to Gavin's office. I'm useless here, worrying about her. I need to do something. Her phone is still going to voicemail, and I don't know what to do next. As I walk into Gavin's office, I discover he's not sitting at his desk. So, I call him. I need him to talk me down from this ledge I've put myself on.

"Hey, Paul." I can hear the traffic in the background. I didn't even check his calendar to see where he was.

"I need to talk. Where are you?" My words are coming out with every breath I take as I pant on the verge of hyperventilating.

"Near our bar. Meet me there. You okay? You sound on edge, mate." I hear the worry in his voice.

"I'll be there in five." I walk at a fast pace back to my office, throw my things together, and head to the bar.

Pushing my way through the door, I see Gavin at our usual table with drinks already waiting. I shove myself into a seat, feeling antsy.

"Jesus, you look a mess." Gavin's brows draw together, his brown eyes full of concern.

"I haven't heard from Soph. I'm worried." I take a sip of my beer, not minding it's still before noon. Gavin huffs a laugh, and my body prickles with irritation.

"Isn't she visiting family?" He sounds nonchalant.

I remind myself that he doesn't know. I'll be breaking my promise of not telling a soul about Sophie's past, but this feeling won't budge. I know deep in my gut that it doesn't matter who she is with. She'd talk to me. We've grown close. These feelings haven't grown out of nowhere.

Gavin leans forward, his eyes scanning my face and my stiff body. "Paul…" His voice is now laced with concern again after taking in my now irritated frame. I can only imagine what my face must be showing.

Sighing, I trust my gut and my best friend and tell him about Soph. Ensuring no one is close enough to us to hear. My hands are trembling as I lift my drink to my lips when I pause a moment, my throat dry from talking without taking a breath.

By the time my glass hits the table, Gavin is on the phone. "Dave, I need a favour. It's urgent." Dave? Who's? Ah! Dave, his friend with a security company. A brief sense of relief hits me as I hear Gavin reel off small details to his friend. Dave is the man he trusted to look after Jess when she was attacked. He's trying to find Sophie.

My eyes start to sting. My friend is calling in favours to find the woman I…Fuck it. The woman I bloody love. My body is swirling with emotions right now; my recognition of my feelings for her has amped up the fear, anxiety, and anger. I'm not angry at Sophie; I'm angry that she could be out there somewhere, hurt, and it's taken me too long to register.

Whilst Gavin is on the phone with Dave giving details of where she was heading, her phone number— just in case he can track it—and the few details I have of Howard and this house in Cardiff, I get up and call her dad.

"Hello?" Sophie's dad answers after a few short rings.

"Is this Shaun?" I try to school my voice so I don't sound rough and then panic him.

"Speaking." He sounds hesitant, but with the amount of spam calls nowadays, I'm not surprised.

"Hi, this is Paul. I'm Sophie's boyfriend." Although we knew, as did those around us, it hits me that this is the first time I'm saying the term boyfriend out loud.

"Oh, hi. Sophie mentioned you on our call not long ago." Although he is polite, I hear a slight alteration in his tone; he's gone from friendly to being on edge.

"This is going to sound a little strange, but is she with you?" I hear the sudden sharp intake of breath on the end of the phone.

"No! We assumed she'd changed her mind and hadn't come. Is she not at home?" I can hear the worry in his voice.

"Shaun, I'm sorry. She's not at home. Her bag is gone, and I've not been able to get hold of her. Do you know where she might be or what could have happened?" Any information could be key at the moment.

"No, no, I can't think of where she would have gone. If she's not at home, she's either at work or with you lately." I know Sophie hasn't divulged what happened in Cardiff to anyone apart from me, and I'm getting more worried every second.

"Do you know anything? When did you last talk to her?"

"I haven't spoken properly recently other than messages about her train details coming home. The last time we spoke on the phone, you were in Paris, I think. Do you need me to come into the city?"

"Not just yet, Shaun. A friend of mine is speaking to someone who may be able to help, but if you hear from her, please let me know. You now have my number. I'll keep you updated on my end. I'm going to find her."

We finished our call, and I felt awful for worrying him, but at least I knew she wasn't there. Other than being in an accident where she can't be identified or abducted by aliens, my only suspicion is that he's found her. I turn to Gavin who is striding towards me and hands me my coat and bag, and we walk to the door.

"We're heading to Dave's office; he's starting the search online and via cameras." He sounds very much like the CEO he is, taking charge of the situation, with no wavering in his voice at all.

"He can do that?" I glance over at Gavin as he lifts his arm in the air, commanding the taxi coming towards us. We hop in and head towards the security firm.

"He can. There's no one I'd trust more with Jess' safety. And now Sophie's. We'll find her." He pats my knee and squeezes to reassure me. I quickly fire a message off to my team to say I'll be out for the day; I left in such a rush I forgot to tell anyone.

The black cab pulls up outside an office building, and we jump out. I follow Gavin inside, my stomach in knots, but my determination to find my girl building with every step. Gavin has confidence in Dave. We will find her.

Chapter Thirty-Three

SOPHIE

I rouse from a deep, groggy sleep, my eyes not wanting to open. I try to stretch, but my body is protesting. What the fuck? My senses come alive quickly now. I hear nothing. I smell mould. My memory comes racing back as I open my bleary eyes to find myself back in the damp room. Fuck.

As I try to sit up, I realise my hands are bound behind my back. It feels sharp, like a cable tie. My ankles are also tied together, which I note is with cable ties. I know I've seen a video on how to get out of these, but I cannot remember how now that I actually need it. I manage to rock myself into an upright position and take in my surroundings.

It hasn't changed at all since I was last here. I do notice a shiny new lock on the door, though. Fear grips me as I realise I may not make it out of here again, or if I do, it won't be alive. My panic rises as I hear movement upstairs, those heavy footsteps near the door at the top of the stairs, and the clinking of locks reverberating around the near-empty room.

As the door opens, Howard's silhouette swallows what light there may have been, like the black hole he is. He's fascinating, charming, and handsome, but when you finally realise you're in danger, it's too late. He's got you in his orbit, and you can't escape. You can only spiral into the darkness with him, all hope and light going as you do.

His heavy footsteps make their way down the stairs, and he turns to face me. A grim smile on his face.

"About time you woke up." The malice in his voice makes me involuntarily shiver. It's the tone he used on me when I was about to get hurt. I know deep in my bones, though, this isn't just going to hurt. This is going to take me to a whole new level of pain where if I wish for death, the bastard will let me heal and start all over again. Torturing me.

He pulls up a wooden chair and sits down; the chair creaks under his weight. I refuse to show fear, but I'm not stupid enough to show bravery. He stares at me, his muddy eyes trying to get through the barriers I have spent years building up. I feel them crumble a little when he leans forward with his elbows on his knees and his hands crossed. He looks like he's posing for a photo shoot, but I know better.

The silent treatment. It used to get me to apologise quicker than anything, thinking my punishment would lessen. It never did. Therefore, knowing my fate, I take a moment to observe him. There are lines on his face that weren't there before. I could mistake them for worry lines, but his face draws down when he's mad; that's probably what's causing those. His face has filled out a little, and his body… He was always muscular, but he has been working out. His arms are bulging in the t-shirt he's wearing; I can see the defined muscles of his torso through the fabric.

His thighs are like tree trunks now. If I'd just met him and was not tied up fearing for my life, I'd be attracted to him. I used to be when we first met, but then he let his personality really shine through. Nothing ruins a pretty face more than an ugly personality, and his is absolutely vile.

His harsh chuckle brings me out of my thoughts; there's no humour behind it.

"Like what you see, Soph?" He winks—actually winks at me. God, he probably thought I was checking him out. Bile rises up at the thought. I push it back down, breathing through my nose, not wanting to risk throwing up all over him.

When I say nothing, he leans back in his chair, crossing an ankle over the opposite knee. Looking very comfortable, whereas I can feel the restraint cutting into my wrists and my shoulders are on fire.

"It took me years to track you down. Very clever not taking your own bag, by the way. I didn't check down here for hours after I got home that night. I'd brought someone back, hoping you'd hear the way she screamed my name. But alas, by the time she left and I came to have you, this room was empty."

My body prickles, feeling the threat building higher. Howard has gone from being as cool as a cucumber, at least pretending to be, to angry, his rage only simmering just under the surface.

"I tried to trace you with your tech, but you're a bright spark and wiped everything. Did you know I'd placed tracking software on your phone and laptop?" He doesn't wait for me to answer, but I always suspected. I'd ditched both at the station I changed at when it occurred to me he could follow me more quickly.

"I went to the train station as a concerned boyfriend, and the lovely young thing behind the desk took pity and helped me find your name for the tickets. Off to Edinburgh, I went. I went to every hotel, coffee shop, and hostel. You were nowhere. After a week of walking around that busy city, it then occurred to me that you could have gone elsewhere. I went back to the drawing board. I searched everywhere I thought you would go. Social media came up with nothing, no matter how hard I tried. You ghosted me, Soph. That hurt." He presses a hand to his chest, but the words coming out of his mouth are like ice.

But his monologuing continues; he always loved the sound of his own voice. "Then, my dear Sophie, I thought about the places you wouldn't go. You never mentioned cities like London, Manchester, or Edinburgh. You said you wanted to stay in Cardiff, Wales with me. It took me a good few years to get to London after searching other cities. I'm only a man, after all, who is trying to get back his girlfriend who said she wouldn't leave. Now, you could have hidden in any of those places I searched, but my gut told me you weren't there. When I finally arrived in London, it only took me three weeks to find you. Good idea changing your name. There are quite a few women named Sophie who work for architectural firms. Now, it did occur to me that you could change careers, but then I know you. I know how much you love architecture and how hard you worked at uni, so there's no way you'd back out on that."

Howard stands, taking two steps and looming over me. I shrink down, not breaking eye contact. I'm terrified, but I don't want to give up hope yet. My reaction causes a sadistic grin to etch on his face.

"So, Sophie dear, did you like the roses I left you?"

Chapter Thirty-Four

PAUL

Thirty minutes. That's the time it's taken between Gavin making a phone call and us sitting in Dave's office looking at a file. The words are blurred, and I can't read them with the feelings coursing through my body. It feels like my usual cool, calm, and collected version has been overtaken by every emotion known to man, all running around at the same time, colliding with each other. I need to get a check on myself because although I'm worried, I need to be focused.

I've had three messages from Sophie's dad and two from her sister. They're both out of their minds with worry and guilt. They honestly thought she'd changed her mind and hadn't reached out to check. When I hear Dave's strong voice, it snaps my attention back to him.

"Howard Thomas. Cardiff, born and raised. Graduated university with an economics degree at the same time as Sophie and has been working locally ever since. There's not much on him, to be honest."

My body swoops downwards, feeling deflated and afraid. If there isn't much on him, then can it be the same person Sophie told me about?

"However, psychopaths don't go around announcing themselves, so the lack of information isn't surprising."

Gavin leans forward after flipping through the file I handed him, which contained a picture of Howard. He looks like a hulk of a man. "Did you find the house Sophie mentioned?" Gavin asks, to which I'm thankful because my brain clearly isn't forming words to speak at the moment.

"Yes and no. We've found a house, but it's not in his name. It's in his grandfather's name, Rory Thomas. The location sounds right." Dave turns his computer screen around so we can see the map he's brought up. The house is situated on its own, off the beaten track, but close enough to the university. Just as Sophie had described.

"Do you have any plans for the house? Does it have a basement? She mentioned a cold, damp and mouldy room downstairs." I don't recognise the voice coming out of me; it sounds so formal and rushed.

"Yes, this house has a basement," Dave announces.

I jump to my feet, catching Gavin and Dave's attention.

"What are you doing?" Gavin asks like it isn't obvious.

"I'm going to get my girl. You coming?" I'm

halfway out of the door when I hear them both behind me. It's going to take a few hours to get to Cardiff, and I don't want to waste another moment.

As we exit the building, Dave runs to the parking garage to fetch his car, reasoning that it'll be quicker than public transport. Gavin is speaking to the police, who, although they are taking us seriously, advise there isn't much they can do at the moment without evidence, and we don't have that. Yet. Gavin takes note of the crime number, and we hop in Dave's car to go find Sophie.

THREE HOURS AND ELEVEN PAINSTAKING MINUTES later, we're pulling off of the main road. Dave had a couple others on his team follow in another car for back up. I'm hoping we won't need it, but without the police here, we don't know what we're walking into.

We pull over into a layby, and I look at Dave in the rear-view mirror, confused from the back seat, Gavin having taken the front seat. "Why are you stopping?"

"This house is secluded. If Sophie is in there with him and in danger, we don't want to announce our arrival. We'll go the rest of the way on foot," Dave says as he opens the driver's door. Gavin gave me a rundown earlier; Dave was in the military in his younger years. He went into special forces after a while, which makes me trust his instincts without knowing him on a personal level like Gavin does.

When we're out of the car, two of Dave's team

members join us, and I recognise them from when they were looking after Jess. Jack and John. The five of us stand there for a moment, and I can feel the cells in my body vibrating, wanting to get to Sophie.

I'm about to start walking—in what direction, I have no idea because I don't know where the house is in relation to us—when Dave pipes up, "Gavin and Paul, you're with me. We'll go to the front of the building, but you two are going to hang back until I say it's safe." Dave hits me with a pointed stare, and I hold my hands up in surrender.

"John and Jack, you find the back entrance." With a nod from the team, we follow Dave.

Trudging through the woods, we finally reach a stone drive that slopes down a hill to what looks like an abandoned house. I mean, considering he was with an architect, I'm surprised he didn't do the place up. But then, who would think about looking twice at this house if they stumbled upon it? It looks in poor repair. I'm surprised it's still standing based on the state of the outside; the paint has all but fallen off, the chimney is crumbling, and judging by a few broken bricks lying around, something is broken. From this viewpoint, I can see that the wood around the windows is completely rotten.

It looks like a house from a horror film, and the thought of my girl being in there springs a new energy within me. I start walking at a faster pace when I feel a pull at my elbow. We're nearing the property, and Dave has one finger to his lips, signalling for quiet. I see John and Jack head in the opposite direction of us, making sure to keep their steps light just like we do as we head towards the front door.

As we near the house, I can see a beat-up old Ford around the side, hiding it from prying eyes. From Dave's research, we know what kind of money Howard has, but then why would you drive a nice car out here? That would draw attention. This rusty, old truck, on the other hand, with its faded brown paint, doesn't look out of place. The car must have been his grandfather's, going by the age of it.

We're standing by the front door, noting that all of the moth-eaten curtains are drawn. No one can see in or out of the house with a clear view. It's so quiet, you wouldn't think anyone was inside. Maybe they're not? Maybe we're too late? Maybe…

Before my thoughts can spiral into a full-blown panic attack, we hear a scream.

Sophie!!

Chapter Thirty-Five

SOPHIE

I knew it! I knew I wasn't going crazy with those roses. The one outside my flat left me feeling shaken, and now that I think back, Howard was all about psychological warfare. It had his name written all over it. Everything starts clicking into place. He must have been around when I smelt his aftershave; he was probably lurking about when I felt uneasy in the changing rooms. He's been there. Watching me.

"How long ago did you find me?" I try to keep my voice steady, although it's raspy from dehydration, and my mouth feels like cotton, thanks to whatever drugs I'd been given.

"I've been following you long enough. You found yourself a nice man there, Soph. Slutting about, buying pretty underwear for him. Although, I have to say I preferred the green on you."

I'm confused, and I know my face shows it; he can't have seen me in the changing rooms. I thought I'd felt off when I was leaving the store, but I would have seen him. It's especially hard not to notice him now that he's the size of a tree.

"Oh, sweetheart, I was always around. I saw that pretty little thing picking out some sets for you, and I saw a green one you'd rejected. Luckily for you, I picked it up." Those muddy brown eyes are almost as black as a predator when he turns to the stairs and picks up a bag with the logo of the underwear shop on it.

Throwing it in my direction, it hits me on the side of the head and falls to the floor. My eyes sting as the corner of the bag grazes my eyelid. The fucker laughs. "Oh right…" Those white teeth are bared as he nears me with a switchblade he pulls out of his pocket. When he presses the button for the blade to flick up, I flinch at the noise it makes. Howard roughly grabs the nape of my neck, bringing himself close to me for the first time since I woke up here. His hot breath grazes over my ear as he uses the knife to cut the tie on my hands. Pain and relief are what I feel at the moment, and I bring my hands round to my front and rub my wrists. Blood is crusting over my skin from the welts caused by the cable tie.

He kneels in front of me and cuts my ankles free before rising to his full height, twirling the blade between his finger and thumb.

"Be a good girl and strip for me." He stands back, eyes now as black as night, and the fear rolls off of me. I don't want to strip. But I also know what comes when I don't obey. My old self is coming to the front, and I can feel myself internally step back as she takes over and does as she's told.

By the time I'm down to my underwear, he raises an eyebrow, and I take that off, too. Slowly. Not to provide a show but to stall whatever is coming next. Howard nods his head towards the bag, and I pick it up, taking out the green underwear. Sage green lace and silk with delicate white flowers over the cups of the bra and the V of the thong. Yes, it's pretty, but it's not me, at least, not the new me.

It's also a size too small; he never could get my sizing right. By the time I've squeezed myself into the underwear, my ribs are struggling to stretch to take in a breath. Maybe he did it on purpose. If I can't breathe, I certainly can't run.

With all my senses on high alert, I hear something outside. It sounds like someone is walking around the house. But I dismiss it immediately. Clearly, my hopes of being found are high, and my imagination is trying to guard me from what is to come. Howard now stands in front of me, his huge arms crossed over his chest and those dark, evil eyes perusing my body like he's got all the time in the world. His tongue licks at his bottom lip as I cross my arms over my chest, inadvertently pushing my boobs higher.

I can feel my nipples hardening through the thin material of the bra. I'd forgotten how cold this room could get, but December in the country can be a little more than chilly. His eyes focus on my nipples, and I notice the erection growing in his jeans. Fuck! I've got nowhere to run. Even if I could magically overpower him, there's no way I can dress and find my shoes before I get out of here. Again. I'm trapped, and I feel my body slump in surrender to the inevitability.

When he steps forward, he uses the flat side of the knife to touch my cheek as he would have once done with his hand. The knife makes its way down to the swell of my breasts, and with a quick motion, he slices across the top. Burning, white-hot pain causes me to scream as my hands fly to cover the bleeding. His hand grips me around my neck, not only cutting off my scream but my air, too. Squeezing tighter, I start to see dots dance around in my vision as I struggle to take in any oxygen.

I hear a bang and thumping above, making my eyes jump towards the sound. I know it's not in my head when he spins his head to look at the door that's flown open. His grip around my neck lessens ever so slightly, and I can just about take a shaky breath. He swings me around in front of him, being used as a shield, feeling the point of his blade in my ribs as his hand tightens again.

Before my vision blurs again, I can see five silhouettes. In my mind, I wish for one of them to be Paul. The thought of him brings tears to my eyes. I'd found my someone, someone I could confide in, who didn't think I was broken. Someone who made me feel, someone I'd fallen for.

When I feel a slight trickle down my side along with the sharp prick of the knife, I hear the words that make my heart burst, even whilst I'm standing in a damp, mouldy room being sliced by my savage, crazy ex.

"Get your fucking hands off of my woman!" Paul shouts.

"The fuck did you just say?" Howard spits back.

"I'll slow it down for you, bud. GET. YOUR. FUCKING. HANDS. OFF. OF. MY. WOMAN. Better?" Paul holds Howard's attention as the other silhouettes move slowly around us.

Chapter Thirty-Six

PAUL

Pure rage is flowing through my body like electricity. Sophie is bleeding, and that fucker has a knife to her side, which has already pierced her skin. She looks terrified, and I want to run to her, but I'm holding back because of the psycho holding her.

Gavin called the police and an ambulance when we heard her scream; I'm hoping they turn up soon because…Jesus! I am not equipped to handle this type of situation. I try to keep his attention on me. Gavin has moved to my side, whilst Dave, John, and Jack have spread out. In my periphery, I can see the three men nod, and I'm hoping they're devising a secret plan to get my girl away from Howard without her getting hurt even more.

Sophie's sob drags my focus back to her. Tears are rolling down her cheeks, and I can see a bruise forming on her neck. My body is vibrating, and I want nothing more than to get out of here with Sophie in my arms.

"How did you find her?" Howard's face is red with anger, spitting the words at me as he speaks.

"Obviously, I'm better at finding her than you are." I shouldn't antagonise him. He appears unstable, but what answer was he expecting?

"Fuck off, you prick. I found her just fine." His grip on her makes Sophie whimper again, and I step forward out of instinct as he presses the knife a little more into her skin, causing her to hiss in pain.

"It took you years to find me, dickhead. Paul only took two days." Sophie is bloody brave talking to him like that with a knife at her side. Howard's face turns a deep red, and it almost looks purple. With a growl, he pulls the hand with the knife back like he's going to plunge it into her, and Jack leaps forward from Sophie's right and pulls her to the floor with him as Dave and John tackle Howard.

In the commotion, I hear the three men shouting, sirens wailing in the background, alerting us to the police and ambulance nearby, and Gavin running up the stairs to show them where we are. I rush to Sophie. Jack is holding her in an upright position with his hand over her side wound, which seems to be pouring blood after her fall. I whip my shirt off and place it around her shoulders to give her some coverage. Jack pulls back slightly and pulls out a handkerchief to cover her wound as we wait for the paramedics.

"I'm here, love. You're safe." I kneel in front of Soph, placing my hands over her cheeks and kissing her forehead gently. But, before I tend to her, I stand and walk over to the three men. John and Dave now have Howard restrained, and the knife is kicked to the other side of the room. I step right up to Howard, who towers over me by a good foot, rear my arm back, and punch him in the stomach, and then with my hands covering his ears, holding on tight, I bring my knee up at the same time as I yank his face down. His grunts of pain make me feel a little better. I'm not a violent man, but apparently, I am when it comes to Sophie. "You'll never touch her again, you pathetic piece of shit."

Howard raises his head, but when he tries to speak, Dave gives him a swift punch to the ribs right before the police come thundering down the stairs.

The paramedics rush to Sophie's side, take in her condition, and patch up her cuts and wounds so she's safe to transport to the ambulance, where the police and paramedics have a lot of questions. I sit by her side the whole time, holding her hand, unable to take my eyes off of this remarkable woman. Her voice is shaky as she recounts how Howard had been following her and taunting her with roses and how she knew something was off on a few occasions. When he finally showed himself to her outside of the coffee shop, he forced her home. He told her he was taking her back to Cardiff, and she refused to go with him. He'd then threatened to hurt her family and me, and when she refused to budge, hoping he was bluffing with his threat, he injected her with something that knocked her out. The next thing she knew, she woke up here only a few hours ago. Her bag was found in his car, making it look like she'd gone away to visit her family. When she woke up, he'd apparently monologued like he was a film villain and forced her to strip and change into under-wear he'd bought her. When she didn't do something he liked, that's when he cut her, and we came crashing in.

When the police were done with their questions, Gavin stepped up to the ambulance.

"You're one strong-assed woman, Soph. I'm so glad we got here when we did." I can see his phone light up in his hand; Jess is calling. He glances down, and with a nod to me, he walks away to take the call.

We're finally alone, well, apart from the paramedic who's tapping away on a tablet and making sure Sophie's numbers are where she wants them to be before we set off.

Sophie's teary eyes find mine. "You found me. I thought I was going to die in that shitty room." Her chest is wracked with sobs. She squeezes my hand and screws her eyes shut; the movement must be causing a new wave of pain.

I try to soothe her, but the painkillers will kick in soon. I hope for her sake, anyway.

"I'll always find you. When I didn't hear from you and those messages—which I'm assuming he sent—didn't sound right, I called Gavin after I'd spiralled a little. Gavin spoke to Dave, and I called your dad. When he said you weren't there and you hadn't been in touch, I panicked. Next thing I know, we've got a secu-rity team, and we're on our way to bloody Wales!" I take a breath, knowing full well I've just spewed a lot of information at her.

"I'm sorry, but I told Gavin about Cardiff. It's how

we found you. His mate, Dave, used the information to find this place, and we drove as quickly as we could to get to you." A new energy has hit my body; relief, fatigue and pure thankfulness are making my eyes sting. The realisation that I could have lost her hit me hard; we were so close to being too late. But the universe, along with these fine gentlemen, didn't let that happen.

The paramedic is happy with Sophie's stats, and we're ready to head to the hospital. Gavin is heading back our way, holding his hand up to stop the medic from closing the doors.

"I'm heading back to London with the team. Let me know what you need and when. I'm assuming Sophie will be kept overnight?" He points that last question at the paramedic, who says it's more than likely. "Paul, I'm also assuming you won't be leaving her side, so you've got toiletries and clothes for both of you heading to the hospital."

"Gav…" He holds his hand up to me, and I feel the tear slipping from my eye as my best friend steps into the ambulance to give me a hug.

"You're alright; you both are. I'll see you when you get back." He steps back out again. Dave and his crew wave as the door closes, and I sit back to look at Sophie again. Her eyes are closed, but she's not sleeping. Her breaths are too shallow.

"Soph?" I rub my thumbs over her knuckles, still not letting go of her hand.

"I'm not mad. I'm glad you told him. It got you

here and us out of there." She is starting to breathe faster, panting, and I look at the paramedic in panic.

She glances between Sophie and the monitor next to her. "Sophie, your heart rate is going up. Tell me what you're feeling." Her soft voice is soothing, but Sophie's eyes fly open, and man, she looks mad.

"PAIN. Fucking pain! Who knew getting cut and a little stabbed would hurt so fucking much!!!"

The paramedic chuckles. Brave woman. "I'll give you a little more of the painkiller, but that's all I can do until you're at the hospital. We still don't know what you were injected with."

The driver tells us we're five minutes out from the hospital, and all I hear is a "thank fuck" from Sophie, which makes me laugh a little.

Chapter Thirty-Seven

When we arrived at the hospital, we'd been in a corridor for a good few hours, and the poor paramedics had to wait with us until there was a bed. Mainly because I was on theirs, but still. It's not the hospital's fault; they were understaffed and had lots of us coming in on the blues and twos.

I was finally checked in and onto an A&E ward about half an hour ago. A lovely older nurse came in with a bag full of stuff that had just been delivered, and I cannot tell you how thankful I was to see fresh clothes, PJs, and toiletries. I know I can't shower until I've been checked over by a doctor, but it's the first thing I'm doing.

Can I eat and shower at the same time? I suddenly realised I was starving, not having eaten since I left London. As if by magic, Paul whips out a giant bag of crisps and looks over to the nurse, who nods before he hands them to me. I'm hooked up to a fluid bag, which apparently hydrates a woman who has been drugged and not allowed anything to eat or drink. Shocking. Damn, I'm cranky, but then who wouldn't be after going through the last forty-eight-plus hours I have.

I rip open the bag of crisps and inhale half the pack, glancing up to find Paul's eyes dancing across me, almost like he's assessing me as I shove cheesy crisps in my face.

"What? I'm hungry," I sputter, still shoving food in my mouth.

"I found a box of Maltesers to go with those." I could honest-to-God kiss Gavin right now. Jess probably had a hand in this, too. I tip my head back in thanks as I hear Paul let out a sigh of relief. I can't imagine how hard this has been on him. Shit! My dad!

"Do you know where my phone is?" The grimace Paul gives me makes my stomach sink a little.

"It was found smashed up in his car. Here." He hands me his phone, and I just let it sit in my hand. Howard never let me near his phone, let alone look at it. And yes, I am very aware the two men are polar opposites, but still, it sets off a spark of emotion in me.

I pull his phone towards me and open up the messages app.

Gavin & Jess: Group Chat: Hi Gavin, Jess, it's Sophie. Apparently, my phone has been smashed! Yippee! I just wanted to say thank you. I'd love for you to come round when we're back so I can thank you properly. But thank you. You saved my life today. TWICE! First, literally. Secondly, whoever put the food in this bag, I want to kiss you xx

Jess: Oh Sophie! Are you okay? Stupid question. Of course, we'll come round when you're back and settled. And you can kiss me when you're back! ;) xx

Gavin: I'll always do anything for Paul, and you Sophie. You're welcome. Ignoring the kissing comment, I'm a possessive man.

Laughing, I open up a new message.

Shaun T & Coral T: Group Chat—Hi Dad, Coral, it's Sophie. I'm so sorry to have caused so much stress. I'm not sure what Paul has told you already, but I know he called you when I was being checked in. I'm okay and will call you soon. I'll get a new phone soon, but you can message/call me on here xx

Coral T: Shut the actual FUCK up!
We're just glad you're safe and we're
coming to see you next week. Paul
said we could stay at his place, and
he'll stay at yours. He sounds an
absolute dream <3 love you xx

Shaun T: Language Coral! And Sophie,
I'm just happy you're safe my love.
Like your sister said, we're coming to
see you next week and I cannot wait
to give you a well overdue cuddle.
Love you xx

Me: love you both more xx

Tears are pricking my eyes as Paul emerges with a bottle of water; I had been so engrossed in messages I hadn't noticed he'd walked off. I hand his phone back, and he rolls his eyes at me.

"Group chats? Really? I can't wait for your new phone to arrive in the morning…" He pockets his phone, and I lean my head back, the day taking a toll on me.

"New phone?" I question, only just registering what he is saying, my voice barely a whisper.

Paul stokes my hair, and I drift off to sleep for ten minutes before I'm woken up by the nurses to check my stats. I go back to sleep, and an hour later, a doctor comes round to tell us the wound across my chest isn't deep but may leave a scar, and the one in my rib only needs a couple of stitches and isn't deep enough to cause damage. I can get the stitches out in two weeks; however, the bruising on my neck will take a week or so to go down, but they don't see any permanent damage.

I'm being kept overnight, which means no sleep and hourly checks by the nurses, but I can go home tomorrow. The doctor gave me the all-clear for a shower, and as soon as the nurses put on waterproof dressings, I practically jumped out of bed. Jump may be exaggerating slightly, but mentally, I jump out of bed. Once they detach from the wires and my cannula is capped, we head to the shower room. Paul helps me shower, being extra gentle and careful around my dressings before dressing me in my new PJs.

Now I feel fresher and less like a mouldy basement. I doze in and out of sleep. Paul stays on the side of the bed and out of the nurses' way, but other than the odd toilet break, he doesn't leave my side. He tosses his phone on the bed when the nurse comes back around and tells me the chats are vibrating in his pocket and doing his head in. I laugh quietly and respond to the messages in between dozing.

The sun breaks into the room about seven in the morning. It's Christmas Eve, and I can go home. I've got to wait for the doctor to come round to be discharged, but I waste no time in getting up to go to the loo. My hydration bag was disconnected around four this morning, so I'm free to wander as long as I don't go further than the toilet. Paul is rubbing his eyes as I swing my legs gently off the side of the bed.

"Morning, gorgeous. We off for a walk?" He yawns and stretches beside me. That chair couldn't have been comfortable to sleep in all night.

"I'm just nipping to the loo. I'll be back in a minute." He eyes me up and down as I stand and round the bed to him. When he stands, he places his hands gently on my hips and kisses my forehead.

"I'll go get us a coffee." He stalks off to the ward kitchen as I head to the bathroom. Under the stark light, I glance in the mirror. Damn, I look like shit! And I laugh as I sit down to pee. What was I expecting?

This is the first time I've been alone with my thoughts since leaving Cardiff. As if on cue, they all come rushing at me. I was kidnapped, drugged, forced to change into underwear he had got me. Not to mention being sliced and stabbed a little… I mean, not how I wanted to spend the holidays. My knees tremble slightly as I'm taking the world's longest pee, my emotions in turmoil as they try to reconcile how I'm feeling. I don't know. I know I'm not scared anymore. Howard can't hurt me again. My body will heal from what he did to me, but being in that room with him brought it all back. I was terrified that I'd die this time; I felt humiliated and dirty when I changed into that god-awful underwear. But this time, I wasn't alone. Paul came for me.

By the time I get back, Paul has wonderful hospital coffee for us. I take a tentative sip, and Paul hums as he drinks his. This is NOT crappy hospital coffee. He pulls out a jar from the magical bag of stuff. Damn, Jess is good.

Chapter Thirty-Eight

PAUL

The sun is filtering through the window of Sophie's bedroom. The dust seems like it's dancing through the air, and the morning light is making her red hair glow like fire. Her blonde roots are showing through more today—not that I care. She's still the most stunning woman in my eyes. But then again, who has time to think about doing their hair when they've been kidnapped, stabbed, and are recovering from said ordeal?

Gavin cleared my calendar and gave me the week off to look after my girl, the woman I love. I finally said the words out loud—over text to Gavin first anyway— that I loved her. He told me to tell her.

So last night, I ordered her favourite Thai food and told this beautiful woman lying next to me that I loved her. Between shovelling pad Thai into her mouth and those gorgeous eyes widening her warmest smile yet had shone through. She told me she loved me, too, and I've been the happiest man alive since.

It's only been a couple of days since she was discharged from the hospital, so we have to be very careful when it comes to the bedroom, but as soon as those stitches are out and she's able, I'm throwing that girl around like a cowboy on a bull. I swear, the minute Sophie said she loved me, too, my body felt like fireworks were exploding inside me. I have always been happy for Gavin and Jess, but I didn't understand the *feeling*. I'd had my fair share of women—more than fair, really—but *nothing* can ever compare to this. That feeling of knowing Sophie is mine and that knowing my previously unbothered-about-love heart belongs to her whilst her heart, that brave, strong, and wonderful heart, is all mine.

Sophie snuggles deeper into her pillow as I move to get up. As much as I'd love to watch her sleep all morning, my body is protesting so much rest. I pad barefoot in my boxers to the kitchen to make us a coffee. I'm staying with her for a couple of days whilst Sophie's dad and sister are in town. I grab my phone and scroll through the notifications. Sophie started a group chat on my phone when hers was broken, but now that she has a new one, she simply added herself to them, and I don't have it in me to leave them no matter how much they ping all bloody day.

I catch up on the thread with Gavin and Jess first, imagining Gavin's delight that he's still in one, too, since the girls talk nonstop.

Then, I move over to the one with Shaun and

Coral. Even though they're currently spending more time together, there is a constant chat when they're apart. Something I love seeing because Sophie spent a long time avoiding contact with them. They talk about future plans, seeing each other more, and there is even talk of her dad selling the house and possibly moving closer to us.

As I sip my coffee, I sputter it out the sides of my mouth as I read the end of the current thread.

Coral: That's not a bad shout dad; I mean the house is quite big for just you in it now. I'll only be a short train ride away.

Sophie: It'd be lovely to have you close by.

Shaun: Well, it's better to move now so I can be closer and ready for those grandkids you're going to be giving me! Haha

Coral: Yay!! Auntie cuddles!!!

Shaun: Grandad, Pops, Grandpa... which sounds better?

Sophie: OMG will you two pack it in? We've not been together that long. Yes, I love him so much...but are we ready for talking about kids and our future?

Shaun: I want a rugby team of grandbabies...

Coral: We're gonna need a bigger
boat...

Sophie: FFS...

I mean, I'm not adverse to kids. I always thought I'd have them one day, but… I take a successful sip of my coffee, not spilling it this time, as I register that after the initial shock, I'm not panicking. The thought of Sophie carrying my child, or children if Shaun gets his way, is actually making me want to go in there and start trying for one right now.

I decide to respond to the thread, hoping it won't freak Soph out when she wakes up.

Me: Gotta wife her up first...

With that, I leave my phone in the kitchen and take our coffees back to the bedroom, where I find Sophie sitting up, phone in hand, cackling like a witch.

"Oh my God! You're gonna make Dad move quicker with messages like that." She places her phone on the bedside table and holds her hands out for her coffee. She's looking brighter, which hospital lighting makes everyone appear paler than they normally do anyway, but since getting home, Sophie has gained more colour, and I'm thankful that her appetite is back, too. But who wants to eat soggy hospital toast?

"How are you feeling this morning?" I snuggle her into my side, mindful not to spill our coffee.

"Better, I can't wait to get these stitches out and be back to normal. As much as I'm enjoying lazy mornings in bed, I want to get back to work." Soph sips her coffee, staring off into the distance.

Gavin called last night. Dave and his crew found some unsavoury things when they were at Howard's house. They shared their findings with the police, and this means he'll be behind bars for a very long time.

In the corner of the room where he'd kept Sophie, they'd found a cupboard. In a black bag, buried under junk, was a skeleton. There were also several pieces of jewellery, items of clothing, and a shoe. Just the one. It seems Howard had either upped his game of wooing women and beating them to killing. Or it could be, which is a thought I don't want in my head, the poor person—we're assuming it's is a woman—was there before he met Sophie all those years ago.

Either way, Howard will not get out of prison for a very long time, and Sophie is finally free. Free of the fear of him coming after her anyway. It'll take time before she's free of him in her head, and I'll be right here by her side every step of the way through her recovery.

Chapter Thirty-Nine

My stitches came out yesterday, and I had my first proper shower without dressings this morning. When I tell you I feel like a goddess, I mean that my entire body has been shaved, scrubbed, and moisturised for the first time in a couple of weeks. Goddess glow happening right here.

I'm standing in front of my bedroom mirror, staring at the body in the reflection. The gash atop my breasts isn't pretty. The pink, raised line is still bumpy after finally healing, and it'll take some time before it fades. There's nothing I can do about it, and I'm willing myself to accept the reminder of survival. Every outfit I wanted to wear today shows it somehow. It's still cold outside, but I can't wear high necks much longer. I'm starting to feel suffocated by them.

I finally settled on my black dress. The reminder is there. I'm also not going to be staring at my own boobs all day, but I accept my scar. My survival is in its pink mark. It's my first day back at work, and although the team has been messaging to say they've got me covered, I can't wait to get back into my projects, my passion. When I fix my hair, I glance at the reflection one more time and find Paul leaning against the door-frame with his arms and ankles crossed, watching my every move.

"You look delicious." He prowls over to me and wraps his arms around my waist, his blue eyes meeting my brown ones in the reflection. I am trapped in his heated gaze as his hands slide around to my hips and hold me with a grip that tells me he wants more. I spin in his arms and cup his face.

"Later," I promise as I grab my bag and get ready to leave. I hear Paul's hum of approval as we walk out the door.

Stepping into the office, I'm greeted with flowers, hugs, and a cup of coffee delivered by Ben. My cheeks flush at the attention, but I'm grateful to be back. When I finally get to my desk, I'm touched by the thoughtfulness of the team. They've labelled my files with different stages of completion and have even bought me vases to keep my flowers in, probably to stop me from using all of the pint glasses up.

Ben comes to perch on my desk, not that there's much space, but he still manages just fine.

"Sophie, we were so worried about you. Paul called me and filled me in when you got home from the hospital. How are you feeling? Are you sure you're okay with being back at work? Not that I want you to leave…" Ben pats the hand resting on my desk as my other lifts the cup to my mouth. Ben bought me a coffee from our lunch date place, which I'm thoroughly enjoying right now.

"I'm good to be back at work, and surprisingly, I'm okay. I mean, mentally? Yeah, that's gonna need some work. But physically and work mentality, I'm good to go." I try to sound reassuring. I am fine. This attention is a little overwhelming, but I'm sure it'll calm down. I hope. Ben knows everything. Paul filled him in after asking if it was okay, of course, but the team only knew the outline. It's not something I want to be ashamed of, but I've hidden my past for such a long time, and I don't want it to dominate my present or future.

"That's good, Soph. It really is. Right!" Ben clasps his hands on his knees and takes a stand. "I'm going to get some emails done, and when you're all settled in, let's have lunch this week."

His charming smile disappears into the kitchen with his silvery hair, and I relax back into my chair. Either my body has adjusted since I've been off, or someone has fiddled with my chair settings. After a minute of wiggling my ass in my chair, I decide someone has messed with the height and back. Once I've gotten it back to how I like it, I open my laptop and crack on with the thousands of emails waiting for me to get my arse in gear.

I'M WALKING TOWARDS HOME, PAST THE CLOSED SHOPS along my road, noting the cute winter window displays as I go. Most of the Christmas decorations are down now, leaving the odd bit of tinsel, glitter and fake snow on the window. As I near my building, I can see my living room light on, signalling Paul is already home. I ended up staying later than I'd planned my first day back at work, but after all the fuss this morning, lunchtime catch-ups, and then finally being able to work through my emails and check the progress of each of my projects, time ran away with me.

I walk through my front door to the aroma of something yummy, my feet carrying my tired ass to the kitchen to investigate and see Paul shredding meat with two forks. The corners of my mouth twitch into a smile that slowly grows and feels like it reaches my ears as I finally work out what we're having. Hoisin duck wraps with spring rolls and chow mien.

"My god, Soph, I can hear your stomach growling from here. Did you eat today?" Paul's back is turned as he dishes up the chow mien and places chopsticks onto the tray to carry over to the sofa.

"Umm…I had some fruit but kinda lost track of time." I download my chaotic day and feel exhausted as I slump down onto the sofa and inhale three spring rolls before Paul has even sat down.

We sit and eat mostly in silence, my occasional foodgasms aside. Paul really is a fantastic cook. I'm chewing the last of my duck wraps after eating four, and I swear I should be the size of a house with how much I've eaten tonight whilst thinking about my future. Our future. I love my job, and the people I work with are wonderful, but the clients aren't always people

I'd choose to work with. They say you shouldn't make rash decisions after a traumatic event, but I can't help but wonder what the possibility of starting my own company really looks like. If I started my own business and we had kids, I could work around them, leaving us less pressure on childcare, which, let's face it, is one of the biggest costs of parenthood, especially in the city.

"I can hear those cogs turning. Talk to me." It's only then that I notice Paul has finished his dinner and has turned his full attention onto me. Those gorgeous blue eyes are sparkling, even in the low lighting of my living room.

"I've just been thinking about setting up my own business. My own architectural firm where I can choose my clients and choose the work and hours I want to do. I love where I work now, but I've done three high-rise drawings recently with very little room to make it eco-friendly or with much greenery." I can feel my heart beating excitedly as I go on, "There's so much more to architecture than making sure the building is structurally sound. It's about creating the space the client wants, creating a beautiful building, and with today's technology, we can make them smart, some even self-sufficient." I feel like I'm rambling, so I take a sip of my drink and gaze over at Paul to see that his eyes haven't glazed over with boredom. He looks interested and as passionate as I feel.

"What's stopping you? You have the experience and contacts, and I'm sure Ben will support your decision and will probably throw in some mentoring, given your relationship with him. I believe you can do this,

Soph. The passion that's just exuded from you in that short time is nothing compared to what I can imagine you'll be like speaking to your clients." Paul stands to take the dishes to the kitchen, which I'm sure should be my job given he cooked.

"If it's the start-up side, Gavin and I could assist if you want our input. I mean, Gavin built this company from the ground up, and I've been right next to him on the financial side. You have support in your corner if you want or need it, love."

I contemplate what he's just said. He's right. I don't know how to set up a business, but I have two people who would help, and I'm ninety per cent sure Ben would advise me, too.

So what am I waiting for?

Chapter Forty

PAUL

It's been almost a month since Sophie went back to work, and if I didn't love her so much, I'd be jealous of how much time she's been spending with her laptop. She's still working with Ben—technically—but I've caught her more than once falling asleep with business name ideas scribbled on post-its and architectural sketches spread out like a second duvet.

She's buzzing. Lit up from the inside. The sparkle in her eye when she talks about her projects, her vision, her way…it's impossible not to get swept up in it. So, when she asked if I could set up a proper sit-down with Gavin, it was a no-brainer. The three of us at the office, whiteboard ready. I even brought pastries. That's how serious this is. I did suggest meeting at our bar for a more informal chat, but with how busy work is for Gavin and me at the moment, trying to carve out that much time out of the office, even if it is for Soph, is next to impossible.

"Alright, Soph, fire away." Gavin leans back in his chair, giving Sophie all of his attention.

Sophie is currently the perfect image of a swan. Above the line of the table, her body is still, poised, and professional. Under the table, however, her legs are bouncing faster than a kangaroo on crack. My lips twitch as she unclasps her hands and opens the portfolio to show Gavin some designs.

"I want to build spaces that breathe and not just another glass structure that meets the building regulations. These buildings will be places people *want* to live and work in." Her voice is a little breathless from excitement as she shows a particular design that has fascinated me for weeks now. Technically, yes, it's a high-rise, but this building has plants all around it. The glass is made from some fancy solar-powered stuff that then powers the building, and it has some futuristic mechanism on the roof that turns the rainwater into drinking water throughout the building. There are even balconies and a rooftop pool. I mean, this is awesome.

"She's got three clients already, Gav. Ones with excellent past relationships with her, and she hasn't registered a business name yet." My chest puffs out, proud of this remarkable woman in front of me.

I'm watching Gavin. After knowing him for years, I can almost always tell what he's thinking. The bastard has his straight face on, but he's impressed. I quickly slide my gaze over to Sophie. She's still swan-like but chewing her bottom lip slightly. It's the only indication of her nervousness that I can see. I feel like I'm at Wimbledon, waiting for Gavin to serve his opinion as my eyes bounce between the two. Thankfully, it is not quite as quick as Sophie's legs, which are still bouncing. Her thighs are going to need a rub later to ease the soreness away; they must be chafing.

After what feels like hours but is literally not even a few minutes, Gavin leans back and gives his charming, white-toothed smile.

"Soph, I bloody love it. Tell me more about your business plan for the next five years and how you'll grow your revenue." Gavin scoots Sophie's portfolio closer to him, flipping through her designs as Sophie lets out a breath before pulling out her financial forecast and growth plans, which I'm proud to say I helped her devise.

An hour later, I'm full of cinnamon pastries and coffee and am leaning back in the chair, listening to Gavin and Sophie talk about her plan. They're currently working on the whiteboard together, and Gavin has helped her tweak her business proposal into a fully functioning plan that is ready to go. All she has to do is decide her business name and set up all the relevant accounts.

"I can't thank you enough, both of you, for your time and energy today. I know how busy you are, and I am so grateful." Soph is beaming as she packs away her stuff and takes photos of the board.

"Honestly, Soph, you did all the hard work. We just added a little advice here and there. All you needed was the confidence to believe in yourself." Gavin walks over to her and gives her a hug; I love the relationship that's grown between them in recent months.

"I'm proud of you and am more than happy to be a silent investor as you start out. It's a sound investment from where I'm standing." Sophie's mouth opens and shuts a couple of times, her eyes tearing as she stands in front of Gavin.

"Gavin, that's such…such an amazing offer. Thank you. I'll think about it if that's okay?"

Gavin says his goodbyes, patting me on the shoulder as he leaves.

"I'm so bloody proud of you." Striding over to her, my mouth touches hers in a chaste kiss.

"I'm still shaking from nerves, and I know Gavin. Can you imagine what I'll be like in front of a big client?" She laughs at herself, grabbing her bag and portfolio, ready to walk out with me.

"Love, you were vibrating on your own frequency. You could have powered this office for hours if you were hooked up to the electricity panel!" I hold her hand as we leave my office, walking to grab a coffee before we both have to head back to work.

"What's next for you? Talking with Ben today?" We scheduled our meeting for the morning, so Sophie could still have her lunch date with Ben. Unfortunately, I have three back-to-back meetings with a small window for lunch, which thankfully, is being delivered courtesy of Gavin's PA.

"Yep." She pops the P, and I know she's nervous about talking to Ben. "Do you think he'll take it well?" Her eyes are cast downwards as if she's done something wrong and is about to be told off.

"I mean, yeah, he's going to be upset to lose you in

his company. But honestly, I think he'll also be supportive. Go." I give her a kiss on the cheek and take a step back to wave down a taxi for her.

"Thank you for believing in me. I love you." She steps towards the taxi that has pulled over.

"Love you, too. Let me know how it goes."

Chapter Forty-One

SOPHIE

Tears are trickling down my cheeks as I sit on our bench, my latte warming my chilly hands.

"Sophie, my dear. I am so happy that you're looking to start your own business. Please don't feel guilty." Ben's somehow warm hand lands on mine with a squeeze. This conversation has played out so many ways in my head, but honestly, he has been very supportive, and if someone were listening to this conversation, they'd probably never guess he was my boss.

"It's been some time since I started up, but I'll always be here for support and advice. You're a friend as well as a colleague." Ben has also never called us his employees, always colleagues, and that is the type of boss I want to be.

"Thank you. I mean, it sucks 'cause it'll mean not working for you anymore, but this is something I really want." I bite into my wrap because even though I've been nervous as hell about this conversation, I am still starving.

"Soph, you're going to be amazing. And from the little bits you've told me, it's already going to be cutting edge and pretty fresh in the market, especially for the UK."

We talk some more about my company, and I feel the excited energy come back, not that it went anywhere other than just under the surface, but it feels great to be buzzing again. By the time we returned to the office, Ben gave me some golden nuggets of advice that I jotted down and was thankful for. He's been in this business for decades, and his experience is invaluable.

As I pack away my laptop and notes and slip them into my bag, I catch my reflection in the glass of the office door. There's still a healing scar across my chest. Even in the colder months, I've been refusing to hide it unless I really want to wear a high neck, but there's also a spark in my eyes that I haven't seen in a long time. Not fear. Not recovery. Just...hope, excitement, and love.

By the time I get home, Paul is already in the kitchen, sleeves rolled up, music playing low from the speaker by the window. He turns when he hears the door, that same grin that always makes my heart stutter spreading across his face.

"Good chat with Ben?"

I nod, stepping into his arms like it's the most natural thing in the world. "Better than I imagined, and my head thought of at least fifteen ways he'd be disappointed, tell me off, or fire me. He was so kind and gave me loads of advice, too."

Paul presses a kiss to the top of my head, holding me a little tighter. "Told you he'd be proud of you."

"Are you?" I ask quietly, knowing the answer because he's told me before, but sometimes, a little seed of doubt creeps into my head.

He leans back, his eyes catching mine with something so steady, so sure. "Sophie, I'm in awe of you."

I smile against his shoulder as I bury myself in the scent of him—cinnamon, coffee, and something that's just home. And at that moment, I know without a doubt that I'm doing the right thing. For me. For us. For whatever's coming next.

Chapter Forty-Two

PAUL

It's a lovely Saturday morning; the sun is out, providing a little warmth in its glow, but the air is still a little cool as we finally come out of the winter months. I've left Sophie sprawled out on her living room floor with designs for her business logo and buildings and filling out the paperwork she needs to set up her business. I'm so proud of her.

I pull my phone out of my pocket and dial Shaun. We've been talking back and forth since Cardiff, and although we've been getting on, I suddenly feel nervous about this phone call.

"Paul, how are you doing?" He sounds chipper today, something Sophie has told me he's not felt for a while. Well, since Betty passed.

"I'm alright, Shaun. How are you getting on with the packing?"

"I hate it. I wish someone could come and do it for me." I laugh; it's a light sound.

"You know you can actually hire people to do that, right?"

"You're fucking with me." When I don't reply, he adds, "Seriously? Do I search for that on the internet?"

"I'll send you some links. You don't want just anyone turning up to your house. Anyway, Shaun, I called for a reason today."

"You asking to marry my daughter, Paul?" His matter-of-fact tone has me stopping in my tracks. This man is a wizard, I swear.

"Um, actually, yeah. I know it's a little old-fashioned calling to ask for her hand, but…" I run my hand through my hair, standing still as people swerve around me on the path. "But I'd love to ask Sophie to marry me. I'd love your blessing, though." My breath comes out rushed with that last sentence. I haven't asked permission for anything in a long time.

Shaun chuckles over the line. Belly-shaking laughter is more like it. "Sophie grew up way before her time, burying herself in studies, and then…well, that happened. After that, she hid herself for years, barely seeing us. As far as I'm concerned, you've brought our Sophie back. She's herself around you, and that's something I thought we'd lost. You are the best thing for each other. You have my blessing, son."

I let out the breath I didn't realise I was holding. "Thank you, Shaun. I'm nervous. I've left her with paperwork and drawings and have come out to look for a ring. But what do you get someone as unique as Sophie?"

After a few minutes of silence, I check my phone to

make sure we are still connected and bring it back to my ear in time for Shaun's words of wisdom, "You'll know it deep in your heart when you see it."

I contemplate his words as he swears at a box that's in his way before he says his goodbyes, leaving me to wander the Diamond District with no clue about what I'm looking for. But I suppose he's right; I'll know it when I see it.

I wander through the rows of jewellers, each window gleaming with rings that all start to blur together. None of them feel right. Too flashy, too plain, too…not Sophie. I step back from yet another window, ready to give up and maybe try again tomorrow.

Then…

Something catches my eye. A glint of light like the sun tapping on glass pulls my gaze back.

It's small. Delicate. A rose gold band with a single oval sapphire at its centre that's hugged by tiny diamonds like little stars. Simple. Beautiful. Unmistakably her.

I barely remember pushing open the shop door or speaking to the assistant, but I leave ten minutes later with a small box tucked into my coat pocket and a thudding heart in my chest.

When I get back to hers, she's still in the same spot, legs crossed on the floor, a pencil tucked behind her ear, lost in thought over some sketched-out building front. There's a smear of ink across her hand, and her brow is furrowed like she's about to redesign the world. I pause in the doorway, watching her. She's my entire world already.

She looks up. "Hey, you've been gone a while."

I cross the room and drop to my knees in front of her. "I had something important to do."

She blinks at me, puzzled. "Okay…" Sophie's head is cocked to one side, her brow furrowed, and she has a tiny hint of trepidation in her voice.

I pull the box from my coat and open it slowly. Her hand flies to her mouth.

"Sophie," I say quietly, heart in my throat. "From the moment you caught my eye in that bar, you've captivated my attention and then my heart. You've built yourself back up from an awful situation, and you've made a life that's yours. And every part of me wants to be in it. I'm in awe of you, and I love you so much. Will you marry me?"

She doesn't answer right away, just stares at the ring like she's not sure it's real.

Then she throws her arms around me, nearly knocking me off balance.

"Yes," she whispers into my neck. "Yes. Of course, I will."

And in her tiny, quiet living room filled with paperwork and half-drawn dreams, I feel like the luckiest man in the world. Maybe because I am.

Chapter Forty-Three

SOPHIE

Six days, nine hours, and forty-two minutes. That's how long Paul and I have been engaged. I keep checking my left hand to make sure that I'm not dreaming.

Do I love him? Absolutely.

Did I think things between us would progress this quickly? Nope.

Did I think we'd drift apart once he saw how much Howard had broken me? A little, yeah.

But he asked me to marry him, and I've been walking on air ever since. The only thing slightly bogging down my energy is that I'm handing in my notice today. I'm going to be working for Ben for the next four weeks, finishing up what I need to do there whilst getting the keys to my new office next week and officially opening the books for SM Architectural Innovations in a month's time. This is downright scary, but with Paul, Gavin, and Ben's support, both emotional and practical and, in Gavin's case, financial, it's happening, and I'm positively buzzing with excitement.

I walk into the office and find Ben waiting at my desk. He knows today's coming, and that our friendship will continue; however, the tug I feel when I see the downturn of his lips is heartbreaking.

"Sophie, my dear." Ben pulls me into a hug, which grabs Richard's attention and has his eyes on us. There's a question in them as we make eye contact, and he's either thinking I'm dying or leaving based on how quickly his eyebrows raise at the sight of my eyes tearing up.

"Soph?" Richard walks over, laying his hand on my back as I pull out of Ben's embrace. I glance over to Ben, who nods.

"I'm handing in my notice and starting my own business." My voice sounds small, so I pull my shoulders back and stand tall. I stand behind my decision, but the guilt of leaving this team is still there.

Richard's reaction surprises me as his mouth spreads into the largest grin, wrinkling the skin around his eyes. "Fuck me, Soph! I'm so proud of you!" He pulls me into a hug that I wasn't expecting, and I wrap my arms around him. Despite our rocky start, Richard is actually a decent human being and colleague.

All of this attention sparks interest from the rest of the team, so instead of dragging out the telling people phase of my day, it's done in one fell swoop. I talked to the team about my business and where my office will be. I also tell them I'd love to keep in touch, which in most cases would have been a lie this time last year, but

I have enjoyed working with them since. Even Crayons, poor Josh. He has improved immensely, but he'll always be Crayons in my head.

The rest of the day passes in a blur of well-wishes, hugs, and the occasional misty-eyed glance that catches me off guard. I expected excitement and maybe a bit of awkwardness, but not this level of kindness. It softens the sharp edges of the guilt I've been carrying.

By the time I get home, Paul is waiting with a bottle of something sparkling and takeaway from my favourite Thai place. We eat curled up on the sofa, laughing about how I somehow managed not to cry in front of everyone—again—and he listens as I talk through every last detail of the day.

A WEEK LATER, I'M STANDING OUTSIDE A BUILDING that smells faintly of fresh paint and floor polish, keys in one hand and a coffee Paul handed me with a wink and a kiss in the other.

It doesn't feel real.

I fish out the small envelope from my bag—the one I've been carrying around for days—and slide the key into the lock. The door swings open with the creak of something brand new and untouched.

The corridor is bright and full of potential. There's a strange silence to it. No humming office lights, no tapping keyboards or ringing phones. Just the sound of my boots on the clean flooring.

I walk down the hall until I reach the door at the

end. The glass panel is still foggy from the morning chill, but as I wipe it with my sleeve, my breath catches in my throat.

SM Architectural Innovations

There it is. My name—sort of—on a door that leads to my office, my future, my risk.

My smile spreads so fast it almost hurts. My heart is thudding in my chest, adrenaline mixing with pride. For a second, I think about taking a photo, but I don't. I want to hold this moment without filters, captions, or distractions.

I push open the door. It's still empty, save for the desk I picked out last month and the swatch book of paint colours I've already changed my mind about twice. There's a folded note on the desk—Paul's handwriting. I don't open it just yet.

Instead, I stand in the middle of the room, arms crossed, letting the silence and space wrap around me.

This is mine. Every inch of it. And I'm just getting started. I finally sit behind the desk, running my fingers along the edge like it's something sacred. And maybe it is. Maybe this desk is the start of everything I've worked for.

Then I remember the note.

I unfold the paper slowly, my heart already fluttering just from seeing his handwriting.

Soph,

Look at you. Your own office, your own name on the door, and that glint in your eyes when you talk about this place. I've never been more proud of you. I knew you could do it. You're brilliant, determined, and completely unstoppable.
Also...this desk? Yeah, we are definitely going to christen it. Just say when. Preferably soon.
Love you more than you'll ever fully believe,
Paul x

I let out a loud laugh—half giddy, half flustered—and press the note to my chest as my head is tipped back, gazing at the ceiling.

Of course, he'd make me cry and blush in the same paragraph.

Chapter Forty-Four

PAUL

Sophie is still asleep when I wake up. The weather is turning, and the warm sunlight is filtering in through the window. Her hair is half across her face, and she has one hand curled beneath her cheek and the other resting where my chest had been a moment ago. I lie there for a while, just watching her breathe like a complete sap, but I don't care. I've never been this kind of man before. Never been the type to linger in bed and think about the future with anything but dread. Hell, I'd not even considered settling down, let alone watching someone sleep. But Sophie's changed that. She's changed me.

It's been just over two weeks since I asked her to marry me, and I still don't think it's sunk in properly. Every time I catch sight of that ring on her finger or hear her call me her fiancé with that smile—yeah, I'm caught off guard, but not in a "panic and run" way. It's in a "damn, I'm the luckiest man alive" way. I'm gone.

Fully gone down the rabbit hole, devoted and in love with this woman.

I brush a strand of hair from her face and press a kiss to her forehead before slipping out of bed. She stirs slightly but doesn't wake. She's been burning the candle at both ends lately, prepping for the handover at Ben's and getting her new office set up. I don't know how she does it all, but I'm proud of her in a way I didn't even know I was capable of. I've not been a bystander, though; I've been right there with her in the evenings, covered in paint and helping her plan the layout of her office. She wants an open plan and no separate office for her. She wants to be fully immersed in her business, and when she gets busy enough to have additional staff, she'll be right there with them.

I make coffee, and then I do something that still feels strange in the best possible way; I text Gavin.

> Me: Fancy a pint later? Need to talk weddings.

Within minutes, those three little dots are bouncing.

> Gavin: Ha! Framing this text. But yes. Text me the details later.

Because yeah, it's happening. We're getting married. And for the first time in my life, the thought of saying goodbye to bachelorhood doesn't feel like a loss. It feels like coming home, and I want to call

Sophie my wife sooner rather than later. Not in a possessive way, but what's the point in having a long engagement when I can wife her up now?

But for now, it's still early, and I make my way back to bed, coffees in hand and a wicked thought on my mind. I place the coffee mugs down quietly. Sophie is still sound asleep, but her position has moved. She's now lying on her back, looking like a fiery angel.

I gently kneel on the bed and slowly lift the duvet. We've been gentle and slowly increasing the pace of sex since she's been out of the hospital, but this morning, I want her to cover my face. I position myself between her legs and hook her thong with my fingers, moving it out of my way. My tongue runs flat over her, causing a little stir, and I harden the tip of my tongue and draw circles around her clit. I lick, suck, and nibble until I hear her moaning in a rough, drowsy voice.

When I feel her arousal soaking me, I tease her entrance with my fingers. Her sleepy, aroused noises are spurring me on, making me want to sink deep into her, but not yet.

"Paul?"

Guess she's awake. I push two fingers in as hers become entwined in my hair, pulling hard enough that my scalp tingles.

"Oh, GOD!" I can feel her walls clamping down on my fingers, but I don't stop. I keep sucking, biting, and licking her clit whilst curling my fingers inside her to find that sweet spot that has her screaming my name. And like I've just pushed the buttons on a fruit machine and won a jackpot, my hair is pulled hard, my name is screamed, and her come is covering my face. I keep going until I feel the last wave of her orgasm before I withdraw, pulling the cover from over us and grinning like the Cheshire cat.

"Morning, gorgeous."

Soph is panting, her body limp from pleasure. "Morning to you, too. That's certainly one way to wake up." Her lips twitch up into a lopsided smirk.

I kiss my way up her body until I reach her perfect lips. With all of the previous women, I didn't indulge in morning kisses. Morning breath is gross. However, whilst Sophie's is still gross, I just don't care if it's her.

My mouth falls onto hers in a slow, sexy kiss. My hard cock rubs against her sensitive clit as her nails sink into my arms. Our kiss turns a little more frantic as her hands move from my arms to shoving my boxers down to grab my cock. She's not gentle. She's horny, and fuck, does that turn me on.

She guides me to her entrance, rubbing my cock up and down, coating me in her come. When I'm right where I want to be, I thrust in, our mouths not parting apart from gasps of pleasure. I know I'm not going to last long; she's already clamping hard around me, and I thrust into her, breaking my kiss to lean back and lift those little ankles to my shoulders to be deeper inside her. Our breaths are shallow and rapid as I push harder, faster, wanting her to come again before I allow myself to do so.

The tingling has started in the base of my spine, so I squeeze my eyes shut and pull up a spreadsheet in my mind's eye, going through numbers as I hear Sophie's guttural moan tear from her, and, fuck me, her pussy is squeezing my cock tighter than a vice. I open my eyes in time to feel and see her come down from her orgasm, and that does me. I'm spilling into her with jerky thrusts before collapsing on top of this woman. My soon-to-be wife.

WE MEET AT THE USUAL PLACE. IT'S EARLY ENOUGH that the pub's still quiet, with just the clink of glasses behind the bar and the hum of the news playing on a TV, which thankfully has the volume turned down low.

Gavin raises a brow as I slide into the booth opposite him, pint already waiting for me. "Wedding talk already? Didn't take you long."

I smirk. "Mate, I've seen what she can do with a Google Doc. I either get ahead of it now or risk being steamrolled by ten colour-coded spreadsheets."

He chuckles, taking a sip of his pint. "Fair. What's the plan?"

"I was thinking end of summer. Gives us a few months to get things sorted, and the weather might not be total crap."

Gavin gives a thoughtful nod. "Nice. Warm enough for an outdoor bit if you're brave. And you're sure about this, yeah? I mean, I like Soph, but this is quick."

It's not said with doubt; it's just that of a best mate's concern that's been there since we were young. The "I've got your back" tone that never goes away.

"Yeah," I say without hesitation. "I've never been surer of anything. I don't feel like I'm giving something up. I feel like I'm getting everything I didn't realise I needed."

He grins at that. "Bloody hell, you've gone soft. I never thought I'd see the day."

"Yeah, well, turns out soft is not so bad. In some cases, anyway," I say with a wink, my mind wandering back to how I woke Sophie up this morning.

We clink glasses, the moment settling between us. A quiet understanding.

"She's good for you," Gavin says. "And you're good for her. Just don't cock it up."

"No pressure then."

"None at all."

We laugh, and just like that, everything feels settled. The date might still be floating, but the foundations are there. She's my future, and I'm all in. I can't wait to get home later and get to planning. She can still have her colour-coded spreadsheets, but I don't want to be a stand-on-the-side groom.

Chapter Forty-Five

SOPHIE

Wedding dress shopping. Just saying the words makes my stomach flip with excitement instead of dread.

I don't think I'll be that bride—the one who squeals over lace and swishes around in front of a mirror, pretending she's in a movie. But here I am on my third coffee of the morning, standing outside a boutique that smells like peonies and expensive perfume, trying to steady my nerves.

Coral's already inside, chatting up the assistant like she owns the place. I love that the relationship between us has grown. I've missed having my sister around. I know I have myself to blame for us drifting apart, but now that we've got this, I never want to let it go again. Jess arrives moments after me, pulling me from my thoughts as I watch Coral. She's wearing a grin that could rival the sun. Paul's mum, Margaret, gives me the gentlest hug as they step inside together. I've only met Margaret a couple of times, but we talk a lot over the phone. Paul is close with his parents, which is wonderful.

I can't stop thinking about my mum. She would've loved this. She'd have made sarcastic comments about the over-the-top gowns, offered heartfelt advice when I needed it, and probably cried long before I ever tried anything on. The bridge of my nose and the back of my eyes sting thinking about her. I would have loved her to be here. Just as I go to take a step, a feather floats down, catching my attention. I notice it's white and fluffy as I pick it up. She's here, after all. I tuck the feather safely into my handbag, push the door open, and focus on the women in front of me. My people.

The assistant, a lovely woman named Ruth, brings out the first round of dresses, and the chaos begins. There's laughter and a few questionable lace monstrosities. In one of them, I look like one of those toilet roll dolls from the eighties and nineties, and there is a short moment when Coral gets a veil stuck in her hair and declares herself "a bridal goddess."

And then the sixth dress.

I step out of the dressing room, heart thudding.

It's simple. Elegant. A soft, flowing silhouette with just enough detail to feel special but not overwhelming. The second I catch their faces—Margaret's eyes welling up, Jess's hands clasped to her chest, and Coral's mouthing *Oh my God*—I know.

Standing on the plinth, I turn to the mirror and see it properly for myself. Not just the dress. Me. A woman who's taken her life back, built something from the ashes, and is about to marry the man who helped her remember who she really is. The dress hugs by body perfectly. I look beautiful.

"This is the one," I whisper. The girls cheer through their teary eyes, and another round of bubbly soon flows as Ruth starts checking for alterations. It fits me perfectly, the only thing needing done is a smidge off the length.

I linger for a moment, staring at myself in the full-length mirror. It's not just the dress that makes my chest tight. It's the woman standing in it. The one who's fought and stumbled and climbed her way to this point. And now, in this tiny bridal boutique filled with laughter and good intentions, I see the woman who is finally, finally ready to walk down that aisle.

I slip back into my normal clothes, which now feel a little rough after wearing such beautiful fabric. *Can I get away with having this material for all of my clothes?* I silently question and laugh to myself.

"Let's go grab lunch," Coral says, snapping me out of my thoughts. "You need food before you pass out from all the excitement, and I need just food in general. Italian?"

I laugh, feeling lighter than I have in ages. As we step out of the store, the weight of the world still sits heavy on my shoulders, but it feels manageable now. I'm not alone. And for once, I'm not overwhelmed by all the pieces of my life crashing together. It feels... right.

These last few weeks have been a whirlwind, and I've been in my own office for a couple of days now. The feeling of owning my own business, sitting in my own office, feels surreal and oddly quiet after working with my old team for years.

I'm staring at a set of pictures and the original blueprint of a building for a new client; this building has seen better days. The structure is broken and abused by years of neglect. But it's beautiful, in a way. It's like a skeleton waiting to be brought to life again. Some of the original architecture is still intact, and it's old, worldly, and historic in a way. The client wants to tear it down and build something completely new. But I see potential…history in those cracks. Magic in the ruin. I want to rebuild, using the original structure. The safety report says it's still of sound structure, so why waste time tearing it down completely when we can reuse what's already there?

My mind whirls, filling with ideas. I can already picture what it could become: a space that blends old and new, history and innovation. The juxtaposition of what was with what could be.

Just as I start scribbling down notes, the door to my office opens, and Crayons walks in, looking slightly nervous but determined.

"Hey, Josh, how are you?"

"I'm alright. You? Can I talk to you for a minute, Soph?" he asks, shifting on his feet.

I sit back in my chair, giving him my full attention. "Of course. What's up?"

He hesitates and glances around the room. "So,

I've been thinking. I know I've still got a lot to learn, but I really want to keep growing. I mean, I've been doing a lot of the grunt work and working on some of the small projects, but I think...I think I could do more. Like, more more, you know?"

My heart gives a little tug. I've seen Crayons work hard and improve, and for the first time, he looks like he believes in himself—when you look past his current nerves. I can't help but smile.

"You're asking to join me, aren't you?" I ask, my voice a little softer than usual.

He nods, his face red with a mix of embarrassment and hope. "Yeah. I don't have a tonne of experience, but I know I've learned a lot, and you spent time with me and helped me grow. I want to keep going. I want to help build your business and learn more from you. Maybe start with one of your smaller projects. What-ever you need."

I sit back for a moment, my fingers tapping the edge of my desk as I think. How would Ben and Richard feel? I mean, I'm not poaching him, and their work is steady whilst mine is growing. I can't do it all myself. I'd like to take some time off for the wedding, honeymoon...I ponder through the reel of questions and thoughts that whizz through my head at lightning speed.

It's a risk, but it's the kind of risk that feels right. He's come a long way, and maybe, just maybe, it's time to take someone on. It's not been long, but I've got a waiting list of a few clients already. I think Josh could thrive in this industry. With a little more guidance, he could handle bigger projects.

"I'll tell you what," I say, meeting his eyes. "You keep learning, keep proving to me that you're ready for more, and we'll see what we can do. You've got drive. That's half the battle."

His grin is wide and bright. "You're serious? I mean, really serious?"

I nod. "Yeah, I'm serious. I'll speak to Ben and Richard; I want to make sure we still have a good relationship, after all."

"Hell yeah! Richard knows I'm here. He said Ben would be okay, but I understand you want to talk to them, too. You won't regret this."

I smile at him, feeling a sense of pride swell in my chest. It's not just about me anymore. I'm building something, and I'm doing it with people who believe in me and this business. Josh hangs around for a while, and we talk about the project I'm currently working on. I'm a little taken aback when he doesn't suggest tearing it down. Some of the little projects I've seen him work on have been all about demolition and building from scratch. But maybe that was his way of showing off his Mickey Mouse drawings. He has vision, and that's something I can be excited about with him.

Chapter Forty-Six

PAUL

I wake up in an empty bed, my hands finding Sophie's side cold, however her scent lingers in the sheets and on her pillows.

I feel slightly disoriented. It takes me a few moments before my eyes open, and I flick my gaze around the room, scanning for her. She's already up, which surprises me, given how much she loves her sleep and how much she needs right now after working so hard over the last few months. Then it hits me.

Why this morning feels strange, different. She didn't stay here last night. Today, everything's happening. I should be anxious, right? Instead, I feel a calmness I wasn't expecting. A certainty. I've been sure of this for a while now. Sure of her.

I drag myself out of bed and shower before heading for the wardrobe, pulling out my wedding suit. The jacket feels heavier than I remember, but maybe it's just the weight of the day ahead. I make a coffee before I dress. It's going to be a long, emotional day. Amazing, but there's no doubt we're going to feel exhausted later.

Buttoning up, I stand in front of the mirror for a second and take it all in: my reflection, the man I've become. This version of me? He's good.

Sophie's not the only one who's changed. I've stepped up and become someone I'm proud of. Not that I judged my bachelor days; they were fun. But this, our future together, has a different feel altogether. And today, I'm going to marry the woman who made all of this possible.

I can already feel the nerves bubbling up, but they're the good kind. The kind you get before something life-changing.

I grab my phone and check for any last-minute messages. There's one from Sophie.

Sophie: You ready handsome? Xx

Followed by a picture of her holding a cup of coffee whilst in a dressing gown that I'm *really* hoping has some sexy-ass lingerie underneath.

My thumb hovers over the screen for a moment before I type out my reply and snap a little selfie with my own fresh cup, making sure I don't capture much of my outfit.

Me: Always ready for you xx

I FEEL THE HEAT OF THE DAY. LATE AUGUST FOR A wedding is beautiful, but we did not count on the good old British weather actually being warm. Since arriving at our venue, I feel my emotions pulling me in every direction as I adjust my tie for the third time. I've never been nervous about anything like this before. It's not like I haven't faced pressure before—hell, my whole career's been built on it—but this? This is different. This is the rest of my life.

I hear a knock on the door, and Gavin's voice floats through the wood. "You ready or need to apply another round of hairspray?"

I take a deep breath, looking at myself in the mirror again. I'm almost unrecognisable. It's not just the suit, the polished shoes, or the tie I've somehow managed to get perfect. I live in suits during the week. It's the guy staring back at me, the one who's about to marry the love of his life.

"Yeah, just about. Let's go get my girl wifed up," I call back, though I can't help the smile that pulls at my lips.

Gavin enters with a grin plastered on his face. "You don't look nervous. I thought you'd be sweating through that tux by now."

"Maybe on the inside," I say, rolling my shoulders as I walk toward the door. "But I'm good. I've never been more sure of anything in my life."

He just stares at me for a moment. I can see the emotions running through his brown eyes, but Gavin says nothing; he just nods as we walk out of the room and head down the hall toward the ceremony. The buzz in the air is electric, and I can feel the weight of everyone's stare, the collective anticipation for the moment I'll see Sophie standing at the end of the aisle walking towards me.

It feels like time is stretching, bending in ways I can't quite understand. Every step I take feels both heavy and light like I'm walking on air. We pass the other groomsmen, their banter and nervous energy a familiar backdrop, but all I can think about is her.

I'm bouncing on my feet, adjusting my tie *again*, and then I see it. The door to the ceremony room, the one that separates me from her. I swallow hard, fighting the lump in my throat. This is it. This is the moment I've been waiting for, and I'm not sure if I'm ready. But I have to be. I want to be. I am ready; I just want her beside me. We've spent so long by each other's side; it's where we belong.

The music starts. Soft, familiar, like a lullaby, and the world shifts just a little. I take my place at the front, Gavin standing by my side, a hand on my shoulder. His silent support is everything. I glance toward the aisle, my heart hammering in my chest.

Then the door opens, and there she is.

Sophie looks more beautiful than I could ever have imagined. She's glowing. Her eyes lock on mine, and for a second, it's just the two of us. She's wearing a simple, elegant dress, the one I'll never forget. I hope it isn't hired because, damn! As graceful and princess-like as she looks, she is also sexy as hell, and I cannot wait to tear it off of her.

I see the nervousness, the excitement, the love

that's always been there in her eyes. She's always been strong, always in control. But now, at this moment, I can see it. She's mine. I'm hers.

I forget to breathe for a moment, but I take her hand, pulling her into my world, pulling her close. And when I speak my vows, it's not just the words I've rehearsed. It's everything. Everything I feel for her.

"You're my heart, Soph," I whisper. "You're my home. You always will be."

And then, as the world watches, we become one.

Chapter Forty-Seven

SOPHIE

The plane touches down, and I can hardly contain my excitement. I've seen pictures of Bora Bora and heard stories, but nothing can prepare you for the way it looks in real life. The water is so clear it almost doesn't seem real; the kind of blue that's impossible to describe. The air smells of salt and sunshine and the promise of something magical.

Paul takes my hand as we step off the plane, his grin matching mine. "Are you ready for this?" he asks, his voice low and just for me.

I nod, squeezing his hand tighter. "More than ready."

The resort staff greets us with flower leis, and their faces are warm and welcoming. We're whisked away in a small boat to our overwater bungalow, and I can't help but feel like we've stepped into another world. The turquoise water beneath us is vibrant and looks like something from a dream.

When we stepped into the bungalow, I let out a breath I didn't know I was holding. The interior is like a work of art—open and airy with large windows that let in the endless view of the lagoon. It's perfect. There are even flower petals over the bed arranged in a heart and a bottle of champagne in a cooler. It's everything I could have ever imagined, and yet, all I can focus on is him.

Paul walks over to the sliding doors and pulls them open, letting the warm breeze flood in. He turns to me, his eyes soft. "This is our time, Soph. Just us."

I smile, stepping toward him. The weight of every-thing—the wedding, the business, the stress—seems to melt away the moment I'm with him. I can hear the faint sound of waves, smell the scent of the ocean, and hear the soft hum of the island. It's the calm after the storm, the peace that I didn't know I needed.

He reaches for my hand and pulls me into him, kissing me softly, tenderly. The world outside disap-pears. There's just the two of us in this beautiful place, and for the first time in a long while, I feel truly at peace.

"Let's never leave," I whisper against his lips.

He chuckles, brushing a strand of hair from my face. "We don't have to. We're here now."

I close my eyes and lean into him, my heart full of love for the man standing before me. This isn't just a honeymoon. It's the start of the rest of our lives together. And I can't wait for every moment of it.

The sound of the waves is lulling my body into a relaxed state. I suppose the exhaustion of the last few months has helped with that, too. Crayon is doing brilliantly and is confident holding down the fort whilst I spend the next two weeks in heaven with my husband. Husband…speaking of, his hands have gone from holding me against him to wandering around my hips, gripping, kneading.

"May as well start as we mean to go on." I lean back from the comfort of his chest to see the wicked gleam in his eyes and the smirk sitting on his handsome face. I laugh as he hoists me up and tosses me on the bed, sending the pretty petals flying everywhere. Climbing over me, the weight of his body settling over mine, I feel the excitement in his shorts. My hands reach up to his face, my engagement ring and wedding band glinting prettily in the sunlight floating into our cabin, and I pull his lips to mine.

His soft lips dance over mine before he leans back. "Well, wife, you appear to be wearing way too many clothes for this activity." I roll my eyes as he pushes himself up and starts undressing me with the finesse of a teenage boy in a hurry. Laughing, I sit up to take off my top and bra. Paul falls on top of me once again after shredding his own clothing in record time and kisses me roughly. It feels as if his need for me is never satiated, and I'm here for it. I feel the same about him. Even when I feel like a mass of jelly after a marathon session.

Paul's kisses roam from my lips, which now feel swollen, to my neck, where he gently nips and kisses his way down to my pebbled nipples. His mouth closes on one nipple, making me pant as I grasp the sheets.

Paul's tongue is circling, and his teeth are nipping as his hands make their way down my body. My legs open more for him, knowing full well what I want. His fingers in me and then his delicious cock.

His fingers gently circle my clit, and I can hear my arousal as he dips his finger into me and then drags it back up to my clit, making punishing circles on the nub. His mouth moves onto my other nipple, causing a fresh wave of moans to escape from my lips. Pushing his fingers inside me, his thumb pad circles around and around my clit, causing my eyes to roll back as an orgasm rushes through my body. I didn't even feel the build-up, but Paul does have a way of doing that to me.

When I come down from the dizzying heights of pleasure, he's lining himself up to my entrance, but I push my knees together and shake my head.

"Are you okay?" Paul's brows are furrowed as I lean up and kiss him, using my liquified body to push him onto his back.

"Your turn." My voice is sultry as I kiss my way down his body. A mix of a groan and growl rumbles from Paul's chest as I near his hard length.

I lick him from root to tip, kiss each of his balls in a deliberately slow fashion, and coat him with my tongue once more before sealing my mouth around the head of his cock. Paul hisses as I slowly work my mouth down, opening my throat to accommodate his length and pulling all the way back with a satisfying pop as I release him. I torture him a few more times with this method before sinking from head to base in one go, gagging slightly when I can't take any more of him.

His hands grasp my hair and guide me in a rhythm as my hand grips his balls, squeezing them the way he loves. Soon, he tugs my hair hard, pulling me off him. His eyes are wide, pupils fully dilated, and I love the sense of pride that runs through me. I did this to him. I wipe saliva from the edges of my mouth.

"Fuck me, Soph. Now!" Paul's voice is hard yet raspy as he yanks me over him. I'm so wet that I sink down onto him in one motion, causing us both to moan boistrously. This makes me even more thankful we have our own cabin rather than a room, and hopefully, our neighbours can't hear us.

My hips are in Paul's strong hands as he lifts me and slams me back down, over and over again, before I feel the pressure deep in my belly, and when I loudly fall, I take him over the edge with me. I collapse on top of him as we both regain our breaths, Paul's hand working soothing patterns on my back.

I lean back a little to kiss him as my stomach grumbles. Paul's body shakes with silent laughter, and he kisses me back. "Let's get you fed."

It's been three months since our honeymoon in Bora Bora, and I can't believe how much has changed. My firm is growing faster than I expected, and we have two buildings under construction now. My team is growing, too. We've added another architect to the roster, and Crayons is officially on board full-time. He's still improving but showing a tonne of promise.

The broken building project I've fully re-designed is beginning to take shape. I can see it every day: metal beams rising, walls starting to re-form where they'd previously been broken down by nature and age. It's not just my vision anymore, though. It's real. And there's something incredibly satisfying about seeing the sketch in my head come to life in front of me.

But as I stand on-site, watching the progress of the building before me, I can't help but feel off. I swallow hard, pressing my hand against my stomach as a wave of nausea rolls over me. It's subtle, nothing major, but enough to make me stop for a moment to steady myself. I take a deep breath, hoping it's nothing more than a bad lunch or the stress catching up with me.

I glance over at my client, who's talking to a contractor, and take a step towards them to join in the conversation as I push any thoughts of what could be causing my nausea aside. It's nothing. Just the kind of thing you ignore when you're this busy. Right?

But then, it hits again, faster this time. I clutch the side of a truck for support, my face turning pale. What the hell is going on? I'm not sick, but this nausea isn't normal. I force myself to focus on the project again, trying to shake it off.

"I'll be fine," I whisper under my breath. "Just stress. That's all."

But my stomach twists again, and I can't ignore the gnawing feeling that maybe, just maybe, it's something more than stress. *Something's changing* is the last thought that flies through my mind as I expel the jacket potato I had for lunch, my breakfast, and what appears to be every carrot in the local supermarkets.

My client sent me home after I apologised profusely about my sickness, but on my way home, I stopped by the pharmacy. First, I need some electrolytes in my stomach after I threw up two more times, and second, I want to grab a test. On my way over to the pharmacy, it occurred to me that I couldn't remember the last time I had my birth control injection. Between meeting Paul, the Howard situation, starting my own business, getting married, and then our honeymoon, I'm ninety per cent sure I should have had one by now.

I run to the bathroom, my stomach emptying itself again. Surely, there can't be anything left, but my body keeps going. I'm thankful Paul's toilet cleanliness is on point as I lean back from the bowl. After the honeymoon, we decided to live at Paul's place and let mine go back to the rental market. It seemed silly keeping two places when he owned his and mine was rented.

When I can finally stand, I wash my face and brush my teeth as I read the instructions. I take some small sips of water, really not wanting to throw up again anytime soon, pee on the stick as instructed, and wait. After setting a timer on my phone for two minutes, I watch the stick as it changes.

Two blue lines stare back at me in under ninety seconds. My hands fly to my mouth as I stare back at them. My mind is whirring with questions. Is it too early to have kids? Is Paul going to be happy or mad that I missed my injection? Do I want kids this early into our marriage and business venture?

The longer I stand there, it hits me hard. I'm growing a tiny human inside my body, and the little bugger is already making its presence known.

We're having a baby.

Chapter Forty-Eight

PAUL

The sun has just begun to dip below the horizon as I walk through the front door. We're entering those darker evenings again, and as I enter the living room, I see Sophie sitting on the sofa, her hands resting gently on her stomach, a smile tugging at her lips as she stares into space. My heart warms at the sight. She's utterly adorable, but a spark of worry hits me as I wasn't expecting her home this early today.

"You okay there, love?" I notice the colour in her face isn't as prominent as I drop my bag and stroll over to her, dropping a gentle kiss on her forehead. She hums in response, but my Spidey senses are prickling. "Soph?" I sit next to her, my eyes scanning her from head to toe. She looks tired and pale but happy.

"So…um. I'm not really sure how to say this, so I'm just gonna say it."

I listen intently, nerves prickling my skin, worry sneaking its way through my body.

"I'm pregnant." She stares deeply into my eyes as those two words hit me like a freight train.

My mouth opens and closes a few times; I must look like a bloody fish before my brain can actually form words. "We're having a baby?" My voice is shaky. I have had thoughts about her being pregnant, about us having a family, but now it's here. Shit!

"Well, I haven't seen a midwife yet, but it may end up being a goat." It shamefully takes me a moment to process those words in my head before I fall back onto the sofa, laughing. "Paul? Is this okay? I mean, we briefly discussed having a family, but I don't think either of us planned it to happen this soon."

I wipe the tears from my eyes and see the worry etched into her face. Is she thinking it's too soon? Does she want to keep it? No, we hadn't planned it, but the universe has handed us a gift, and I am not going to step down now. I'm her husband, and I'm going to be a dad.

Fuck, I don't know what to do with kids! I'm going to be a dad!

I take her hands in mine and seat myself so I'm facing her head-on. "Soph, of course, this is okay. Unexpected? Yes. Unwanted? Fuck no. We're having a baby." My voice is soft, and I lean in to kiss her as her face turns a worrying shade of green, and she lurches off of the sofa and into the bathroom. I race after her, holding her hair and rubbing circles on her back, hoping I'm soothing rather than being annoying.

The to-do list I came home with in my head is

scrapped. The first thing I'm doing is looking up what the fuck to do next.

"No. Nope. What even is that? No. No." Gavin is having a great time scratching off items from a list I found on the internet. Apparently, when you search "What do I need when having a baby?" you get a fuck tonne of suggestions you don't need. Thankfully, with Gavin and Jess recently adopting, they have some experience in this whole raising-kids-without-killing-them thing.

"Are you leaving anything on there?" I peer at the sheet of paper that had over a hundred suggestions and now only has about twenty items.

"Yep. Everything you *need*. Anything else Jess and I have. I can't believe you're gonna be a dad." He looks up at me as he hands over the piece of paper. I know he doesn't mean he *can't believe it*, but let's face it, this last year or so has been…a huge change for me.

"Honestly, I'm terrified. But I'm also full of excitement and wonderment that Sophie is growing an actual human inside of her, and I want to be prepared."

Gavin laughs lightly. "Mate, you can be prepared as you like, but once this kid comes, those lists, preparations, things you think you're gonna do are all out of the window. Trust me." Well, that's helpful. "One thing you may want to think about, though, is a house. You might not want to just yet, but when they start to walk, they'll want to be outside in a garden—when the weather permits—and not cooped up in your apartment."

And there's another thing to add to my list to talk to Sophie about. Gavin and I finish up, and I go home to see my wife. She's over three months pregnant and has just popped. I can't keep my hands off of her stomach where our tiny human is growing. Neither of us care if they're a boy or girl, we just know how much we already love them.

As I walk in, Sophie is sitting in a crop top and tiny shorts. She's apparently one of those women who are constantly hot during pregnancy and strips down to basically nothing when she's not in the office. I'm also increasingly thankful that her hormones have sorted themselves out, and she's not throwing up anymore. They have, however, increased her sex drive to the point my dick may fall off before this baby comes, and they may end up being an only child.

Am I complaining? Fuck no.

Am I willing to help her through any part of this pregnancy? Fuck yes. So here I am, falling on my sword, as those brown eyes find mine and give me a knowing look. I dump my bag, coat, and shoes, winking at her as I pad over to where she's now standing. Taking her gorgeous face in my hands, which thankfully is back to her normal colour with an added pregnancy glow, I plant my lips on hers in a deep, meaningful kiss.

With her hands threaded into my hair, pulling me in deeper, I hoist her up and carry her into the bedroom as she wraps her legs around my waist.

I can't leave her in need; after all, she's my wife. And when my wife is horny as fuck, I shall deliver.

Epilogue

SOPHIE

The office hums with the soft clatter of keyboards and the murmur of brainstorming sessions. I lean over the desk, smiling warmly at Andrea, my intern who is carefully taking notes as I talk her through a small project we've been asked to draw up. My business is thriving since Josh joined, and I now have a team of four as well as Andrea, who will be working with us all whilst she's studying for her qualification.

I can see the spark of ambition in Andrea's eyes. It feels like she's trying to soak in every word I say and every stroke of my e-pencil as I draw. She reminds me of the young Sophie back in the early days before I fell for Howard. "You're almost there," I say gently, guiding her hand to adjust a design on the screen. "It's all about the details. Don't rush them."

Josh—the name Crayons was long ago abandoned because he has flourished over the years—comes over to us. He's one of my senior team, and honestly, a damn fine architect with a great vision.

"Time, Soph." He nods his head to the clock, my eyes following. Shit! I've left it a little to the line today. I hand over what we're doing and leave Andrea with him. I grab my bag and head to the nursery.

I get there at bang on five and see Theo's big blue eyes watching me as I sign in. He is essentially a tiny version of Paul with his eyes and floppy dark hair. How did I carry him for nine months for him to end up looking like his dad? My arms open wide as Amy, his key worker, tells me about his day.

"Oof." My breath is almost knocked from me as my big boy runs into my body with zero finesse or coordination. But what do I expect from a three-year-old?

"You had a good day, baby?" I hold onto him tightly, feeling like he's growing up too quickly for my liking, but after taking time off with him and then wanting to go back to work and feeling guilty about him going to nursery, I wouldn't change any of it. He absolutely loves it here. It's a forest nursery, so he spends a lot of time outside, immersing himself in nature and learning all sorts of wonderful things.

"Trucks!"

Amy laughs as he runs off to get his bag. "We've been making tracks with paint and truck wheels today. He's thoroughly enjoyed getting messy. Hence, the change of clothes. Twice." I love that he enjoys messy play. My washing machine, however, may need help catching up with the amount of clothes we go through daily.

When we get home, I can see Paul's car in the driveway. After we had Theo, we stayed in the apartment for six months before deciding we needed more space. The baby stuff alone was crammed in, let alone the additional bits we needed to get as he grew. So, we bought a house in the countryside not, too far from Jess and Gavin. Their children, Harry and Bella, are absolutely besotted with Theo. It makes my heart warm. Jess's friend Kiera isn't far away, either, with her husband Ed. They're starting a brood of their own.

I saunter into the garden after taking my shoes off and find Paul putting the lawn mower away. Who knew you could find that attractive in a man? But then again, his skin is glistening with a light sheen of sweat in the sunshine. As if feeling the weight of my stare, he turns and drops down to one knee with his arms open for Theo, who rushes from my side down to his dad. I love their bond. Paul was very hands-on when Theo was born, and we decided to bottle-feed him so that he could share those bonding moments with his son, too. Honestly, I enjoyed getting a little extra sleep. Who wouldn't with a newborn?

Theo is chasing Paul around our back garden, and I take a seat in my comfy chair as I watch, deep in thought.

My life has certainly had its ups and downs. Losing my mum, whose feather that dropped on my dress shopping day, which I keep in a glass orb in the living room window, university and the shit storm that happened there, moving to London and estranging myself from my family…something that definitely isn't a problem now. I see my sister every two weeks, and my dad is here most days. I'd like to say for me, but we all know he's here for his grandson, and I love it. I love that we've regained our relationship after the years I kept us apart.

Then I met Paul, and my world turned upside down. I cannot see my life without him, and I will be forever grateful that he was in the bar that night. My hand falls to my stomach, rubbing gentle, protective circles. I glance down and whisper to my stomach as I hear Theo squeal and giggle. "When he's finished playing with your brother, I'll tell Daddy about you."

I found out this morning that we're expecting number two, and my heart is filled with so much joy that it has taken all of my effort not to call Paul and tell him. I wanted to see his face when I told him our family was growing.

I glance up at the garden and can't see the boys, or more concerning, I can't hear them. I straighten my back to see if they're around, and then I hear a tiny giggle from behind my chair. I close my eyes and feel the smile spreading across my face, not wanting to spoil his scare opportunity.

"BOO!!" Theo's tiny voice shouts as he jumps to my side.

My hand flies to my chest, and I feign shock. "AHH!" I giggle and scoop him up into my arms. I turn my head to find Paul leaning up against the garden table. His eyes are skimming over me. I set a wriggling Theo down, who runs off immediately, and Paul stalks over to me, dropping down to his knees beside my chair.

"What exactly are you going to tell Daddy?" His eyes meet mine as his hand rests on my stomach. I bite my bottom lip as I nod at him, eyes welling. Paul simply lifts his hand to pull my lip free and kisses me. Ferociously.

Leaning back, I try to gauge his reaction, already knowing he's going to be happy. We've talked about having two kids since we found out about Theo. Paul's eyes soften the moment our lips come apart. It's as if time itself has paused, and we savour this moment together. His lips part slightly, a soft breath escaping as his gaze locks with mine, and the corners of his mouth lift, but it isn't just a smile. It is a smile that speaks of pure adoration, of awe, as though the world has just shifted into a perfect place. His hands reach for mine, gently pulling them into his own as his eyes shimmer with the kind of love only a man who has truly known a deep devotion.

"I can't bloody wait. Although," he glances down at his jeans and then back at me, his eyes sparkling, "we may have to get to practising for that pregnancy horniness you get." And with that, he smashes his lips against mine, devouring every piece of love I have and giving everything right back.

Epilogue Two

PAUL

A few years ago, my life was having a different woman in my bed each night, working with my best friend, and generally living the carefree life of a young bachelor.

I had an amazing life, or so I thought. That was until I met her, and my life tilted on its axis.

Now, I'm happily married to the most wonderful, gorgeous woman in the world, and we have two amazing children who drive me up the wall. To the point of madness some days. Then they wrap their tiny little arms around me and say "I love you, Daddy" in the sweetest voice, and fuck me if my heart doesn't melt every. Bloody. Time. And, of course, I still get to work with my best friend and his wife.

We have a house in the countryside, and although my life has changed from expensive suits, meals, and anything I wanted to still expensive suits that now have to be dry cleaned more often because of tiny messy hands, and expensive meals because who knew kids ate this much? And I have everything I want right here.

All because I went to the bar one night, I met Sophie, and something inside me knew that I was going to end up falling for Red.

Acknowledgments

To my readers, I love writing and creating stories. The fact you enjoy them, honestly, makes my heart smile and I give a little happy dance with each review I read, so thank you for reading, enjoying my characters, their quirks and leaving your reviews. It honestly means the world to me.

The patience in waiting for this book has been outstanding, unfortunately, as a lot of you may understand, grief took over and writing ceased for a good six months. It took a while to get back into the swing of things, but I'm also thankful I took that time. Our mental health is so important and taking the time to heal after such a loss, gave me back the energy I needed to finish this story.

Thank you to Tracey, Maria and Gareth—You guys provide such great feedback and have supported my love in writing, motivating me capture my imagination in these books.

To my cousin, Coral, you like every post—on every platform—you read each of my books and share most of my socials too. Your support does not go unnoticed and I am so grateful. Love you babes, you now have a character named after you xx

To my local Starbucks, you guys have fuelled my energy and provided me with not only a great office to work from when I need to get out, but friendly smiles and conversation. You are awesome people, and I love that you're a part of our community.

And finally, my husband. Who, two years after I published the book, has finally picked up Falling for the CEO and is thoroughly enjoying it. You are my rock, my sounding board, my soul mate. You support my dreams, and I will be forever thankful for you. Together, we are showing our demons what a dream team looks like. You and me baby, forever and always xx

About the Author

Hi, I'm Elenor Pountain [pon-tain].

Living in The Midlands, UK, I'm an avid reader who loves devouring books in her spare time and a hopeless romantic with a dark, sarcastic humour. I'm a mum of 2 energetic daughters (who I call my demons on socials) and 2 lively black labradors as well as a wife to my best friend and husband.

I write steamy contemporary romances where the story lines are realistic and relatable. I enjoy making my characters come to life in my stories, and then watching as they take it over, sometimes changing the plot completely. In each of my books, there is a part of me in there, whether it's in the humour, the experience or just a sarcastic comment.

I hope you enjoy reading my books as much as I enjoyed writing them.

Website - elenorpountain.com
LinkTree - linktr.ee/86ep

instagram.com/elenorpountainauthor

tiktok.com/@elenorpountainauthor

amazon.com/author/elenorpountain

<u>FALLING SERIES</u>

Falling for the CEO (#1 of the Falling Series)

Falling with Kiera (#2 of the Falling Series)

Falling for Red ((#3 of the Falling Series)

Dark Romance series coming soon…

www.ingramcontent.com/pod-product-compliance
Lightning Source LLC
Chambersburg PA
CBHW050440200726
48295CB00024B/745